FROM THE GROUND UP...

The man in the vest charged toward Clint like a bull with its head lowered for the gore. Clint stepped forward. Grabbing the other man's shirt between the collar and shoulder, he used the fellow's momentum against him and pivoted on his heels while pulling back. The combination of the speed in the gent's steps, along with Clint's redirection, diverted the bull's charge and sent him face-first into the side of the passage.

Already turning his attention to the door, Clint held his Colt at the ready while shoving the man in front of him straight down to the floor. When the man in the vest hit the ground, Clint stomped his boot down between his shoulder blades.

A second man was on the way. The first, although dazed, was still trying to get onto his feet. Clint pressed his foot harder into the other man's back. A shot blasted through the room, its thunder growing into an explosion in the corridor. Squirming, the man with the vest struggled to get out from under Clint's leg. Before he had to worry about that one, however, he saw a shadow—then the muzzle of a gun as the light bounced off the dull metal.

Clint thought the other man was running to his friend's aid, but apparently Cam had thought twice before making the same mistake as the man in the vest. Cam pulled his trigger.

THE GUNSMITH

258

THE RAT'S NEST

J. R. ROBERTS

JOVE BOOKS, NEW YORK

This is a work of fiction. Names, characters, places, and incidents either
are the product of the author's imagination or are used fictitiously,
and any resemblance to actual persons, living or dead, business
establishments, events, or locales is entirely coincidental.

THE RAT'S NEST

A Jove Book / published by arrangement with
the author

PRINTING HISTORY
Jove edition / June 2003

For information address: The Berkley Publishing Group,
a division of Penguin Group (USA) Inc.,
375 Hudson Street, New York, New York 10014.

ISBN: 0-515-13550-X

A JOVE BOOK®
Jove Books are published by The Berkley Publishing Group,
a division of Penguin Group (USA) Inc.,
375 Hudson Street, New York, New York 10014.
JOVE and the "J" design
are trademarks belonging to Penguin Group (USA) Inc.

PRINTED IN THE UNITED STATES OF AMERICA

10 9 8 7 6 5 4 3 2 1

ONE

No matter what else he might have been known for, Clint Adams thought of himself as a craftsman. Although just as many people knew him as the Gunsmith as they knew him by his given name, those same people mainly thought of that as just a title. They thought of him as a gunfighter above all else.

That wasn't Clint's preference. It was just the way his hand had played out.

But Clint knew what it was like to make something with his own two hands. He knew the feeling of building something that not only worked, but worked better than if someone else had been assigned to the same job. In fact, the modifications he'd made to his own Colt had saved his life more times than he could easily count.

Whether it was a piece of the weapon's mechanism that was delicately filed down or a new twist on the gun's firing system, that Colt was truly unique. Of course, the hand wielding the weapon was just as important and when those two elements were combined, truly amazing things could happen.

Separating oneself from the gunfight itself, one might say that the Colt worked like a piece of art. After so many

1

years of carrying the pistol and making it his own, Clint felt like that gun was a part of his own hand. It molded to him as though it had been created with only him in mind and in some ways . . . it had.

Yes, Clint Adams could appreciate fine craftsmanship.

The only time he didn't like to see such care taken in someone's work was when that work was used against him. Holding his head down low because he couldn't raise it up any higher, Clint had to smirk at that thought. He figured many of the men who'd tested their steel against his own Colt probably thought the same thing. After all, no animal is going to stop and admire the fine quality of the trap that was chewing into its leg.

In that respect, Clint felt like he could relate to the other side of that analogy much better. He reflexively tensed the muscles in his arms and shoulders, unable to do much more than shift less than half an inch in any direction.

Rough, splintered wood gouged into his back, making little tears in his sweat-stained shirt. It didn't feel comfortable, but at least it was something he could feel since much of his upper body had started going numb some time ago.

Clint didn't know how long he'd been there. A new watch was in the front pocket of his jeans, but there was no way for him to reach it. In fact, he could even feel the weight of his modified Colt hanging at his side, but he knew better than to look down for it. The weapon wouldn't be there. Whatever he felt was the same as the phantom pain of a man who was missing an arm or leg.

His brain was so used to the pistol being there that it still let him feel the sturdy leather holster resting on his hip. But the Colt wasn't there. Clint knew that for certain. Simply thinking about where it might be was enough to get his blood flowing through his veins and his heart pounding in his chest.

With the surge of energy, Clint felt a surge of emotion

as well. He couldn't let himself be kept there any longer. If he could just pull up some more strength from the bottom of his soul and pour it into his muscles, he might be able to break something loose. Even if it was just a tiny crack in one of the metal rings holding his wrists, or a piece of the wooden rack holding those rings . . . any break at all was all he needed.

Clint ignored the pain in his chafed wrists and the stabbing sensation in his back as he battered himself again and again upon the sturdy planks behind him. Although it felt like he was making some degree of progress, Clint was only able to get about a quarter of an inch between his back and the wooden slats before slamming against them with all his strength.

After what felt like an eternity but really was less than a minute, Clint pounded himself one more time against the wood and let what was left of his energy drift away. Standing with his boots against the ground and his back stooped forward, he needed some of his energy to keep himself from hanging with all his weight against his restraints.

His wrists were still bound to the wooden door with his arms held out to either side as though he was being crucified. The apparatus holding him in place was simple, yet elegant in its design. Thick, iron rings circled his wrists and were held in place so tightly that all of Clint's fighting had yet to loosen them in the slightest.

His neck was bound by rope that was also tied to the apparatus behind him and the whole thing was bolted to the underside of a door that opened up from a small root cellar. The cellar itself wasn't quite big enough for Clint to stand upright even if he was able to move about at his leisure. Where the door was, Clint would have had to bend his head and stoop forward to keep from knocking the back of his skull against the sturdy wood.

But after he'd been locked inside his restraints, with his

shoulders and arms held firmly in place, Clint was forced to stand on his tiptoes due to the odd angle of his body. The rope around his neck was just tight enough to cut off his circulation if he relaxed his legs for too long. And since he didn't know if his captors had any intention of coming back for him, Clint had the unsavory choice of starving to death or hanging himself.

All in all, it wasn't a choice he was too fond of making.

Hanging from the rings as much as his circulation would allow, Clint took a few deep breaths and tried to regain some of his strength. As he did, he craned his neck for a look around the cellar, just in case there was something he might have missed the other times he'd surveyed his surroundings.

The only light that came into the musty space was what little sunlight made it through the cracks in the door. Clint was very familiar with those cracks since he'd been watching those slender rays of light for any hint that his efforts were splitting the boards any farther apart.

Although the door shook beneath his assaults, the boards had yet to crack apart enough for the slightest bit of hope to take root in Clint's mind. Once again, the notion of sturdy craftsmanship came to his mind. If nothing else, at least the person who put that door together sure knew what he was doing.

When Clint laughed silently beneath his breath, it sounded like a hoarse cough instead of anything that might reflect the least bit of joy. He shook his head, amazed that he could be even somewhat amused at a time like this. But it was either laugh or fall into a darker emotion and when every second was precious, there simply wasn't much time to spare for the darker emotions.

Clint shifted once again, slowly grinding his back and shoulders against the door and the contraption bolted to it. The rack holding him in place didn't move in the slightest. If he shifted too much in the wrong direction, he could even feel the rope cut into an artery on the side of his neck, causing dark splotches to dance behind his eyes.

If he kept that up, he would pass out.

And if he passed out, there was the very real possibility that he might never wake up.

Needing to give himself a couple moments' rest, Clint positioned his body in the way dictated by the rack bolted to the underside of the cellar door. Conforming to the device felt like defeat and a searing knot formed in the pit of his stomach, but he stood there anyway.

He was too tired to fight for the moment, but his mind was racing faster than a rabbit with a hound nipping at its tail. Part of his thoughts were on getting himself out of the finely crafted rack, while the other part reminded him of what had gotten him strapped there in the first place.

TWO

The sun had been riding in the sky like a peacock strutting to show off its feathers. All of the recent dawns had been glorious events and the end of the day had been no less splendid. The dusk had been a wash of dark hues of purple and red, which reminded Clint of just how different it was to be making his way across the western prairies of Nebraska and Kansas.

After wrapping up a small matter in Kansas, Clint had decided to head northwest simply because he hadn't been in that part of the country for a while. He was no stranger to wandering without a grand scheme in mind. In fact, he rather preferred it.

Clint lifted his nose to an oncoming rush of wind, closed his eyes, and imagined what it would be like to be tied down to any one place for any extended amount of time. Sinking roots somewhere with a decent view had its appeal, but only if he were to be transformed into another person. Like any other man who went where the wind took him, Clint entertained thoughts of a homestead or ranch outside of a town where everyone knew his name. There would be a woman who cooked for him and shared his bed and there would always be wood that needed to be chopped whenever he had nothing else to do.

When everything else was done, he could sit on his porch and drink in the sight of the sun as it sank slowly beneath the horizon. Such a sight would have been no less glorious than the one he saw from the back of his Darley Arabian stallion. In fact, without Eclipse nearby, Clint would feel somehow less complete. Like the black horse, Clint's legs needed stretching every now and then, pure and simple.

There was no rhyme or reason. That was just the way he was made. He was too set in his ways to change them and knew better than to tempt nature by trying.

As he rode across the prairie, Clint let his mind wander along those paths as his eyes soaked up the setting sun. It would be dark before too long and he needed to find a good place to set up camp. Eclipse probably could have ridden all through the night, but rather than put that to the test, Clint decided to keep up his leisurely pace and find a clear spot next to some source of wood.

Darkness crept over the landscape, enveloping Clint as he walked in a circle around the spot he'd tied off Eclipse and picked up promising chunks of firewood. By the time the stars could be seen overhead, flames jumped amid a pile of branches and Clint sat back just to watch them burn.

The motions of preparing his meal and brewing some coffee were so worn into his system that Clint didn't even have to think about what he was doing. Instead, all he did was let himself go through those motions and enjoy the fact that he didn't have to put any energy into it.

Clint leaned back on his bedroll and let sleep overtake him. All in all, the day was merely a simple matter of traveling from one point to another and taking care of his basic needs. But even so, it felt like he'd indulged himself somehow. There was a calm, peaceful feeling in his chest that he figured must be what those other people felt after putting in a hard day's work on that ranch he'd dreamt about.

Not that Clint was a stranger to a hard day's work. He'd poured out enough blood and sweat to supply a river in his lifetime, but he'd always packed his things and moved on soon afterward. For him, the open range was his porch and the ground was his bed.

The occasional hotel room was well and good, but it was never home.

"Here," Clint thought as he folded his hands over his chest and stared up at the sky sprawled out above him. "This feels like home."

Those same stars looked down at him no matter where he traveled and the same sun would be there to wake him up when it was time to rise.

Comfortable in his element, Clint closed his eyes and let himself drift off to sleep as a stray breeze rushed over his face and down over the entire length of his body.

He awoke just before dawn and was back on the trail less than an hour later. The leftover coffee had been cold and the trail mix was less than a step away from being stale but it was enough to get him ready for what was ahead the next day. It wasn't until he'd started riding that he decided to make his way up to the Badlands of South Dakota.

The natives there would see him coming and might decide to throw him a welcoming party, but Clint knew enough names and was owed enough favors among the Indians to alleviate any concerns in that area. Now that he had a destination in mind, Clint figured the path he would take to get there.

To the best of his recollection, there were a couple towns along the way that might be worth visiting. Some of the bigger ones were North Platte, Nebraska, and of course Rapid City, South Dakota. It had been a while since Clint had traveled along that route, but he was also certain of a few smaller towns that would be good to stay for a night and re-supply. Of course, with towns that small, there was just as much of a chance of them booming or disappearing altogether.

Well, since Clint was in no big hurry one way or another, he chalked up that gamble to one of life's pleasant uncertainties. That was the kind of mood he was in as he rode north toward the Nebraska panhandle. With the buffalo herds long gone and the wagon trains becoming something seen only every so often, there wasn't a lot to see along that trail. For the better part of a day, Clint could have safely fallen asleep in his saddle without worrying about coming across anything that needed his attention.

The funny part was that he was perfectly happy with things remaining nice and boring.

Toward the end of the next day, he spotted a jagged row of buildings on the northern horizon. He'd been fairly certain that a town was nearby and when he saw the structures, he wasn't at all surprised. The only thing that troubled him in the least was trying to decide if he would sleep in a bed or under the stars that night.

He smiled to himself, feeling rather pleased to have such a trivial thing at the top of his concerns.

THREE

Looking back at that moment, Clint felt like he'd made a mistake in allowing himself to get so relaxed. After all . . . weren't those the times when things always came crashing down? Weren't those always the times when men were put in their place for daring to think that they had such a firm handle on their situation?

They certainly were.

If Clint had learned anything after years of fighting his way out of one trial and landing squarely into another, it was not to let your guard down. That didn't mean that he wasn't allowed to be happy. Hell . . . Clint didn't even really know what it meant. All he knew was that looking back upon the past wasn't always a good thing to do.

Although, since he was hanging by his neck and arms from the underside of a door to a root cellar, he didn't have a whole lot of other ways to pass his time. While his mind went through its paces, Clint's body went through its own as well.

For the moment, he'd given up on trying to break the rack that held him. Instead, he merely flexed his muscles as a way to keep himself limber and ready for when his opportunity to move finally came. Clenching his fists and keeping his eyes trained straight ahead, he slowly pushed his arms forward until the steel rings bit too deeply for him to bear.

As far as he could tell, his skin wasn't too badly damaged. The last thing Clint needed was to start bleeding. That would only have made him more tired in less time. Tensing the muscles in his jaw, Clint worked his head back and forth and from side to side, testing the rope around his neck in every direction.

He could smell the sweat oozing out of him. The scent was only amplified by the close quarters of the cellar, which also made every one of his motions echo like thunder in his ears. To take his mind off the pain, which grew and grew the more he went through the torturous regimen, Clint focused on another part of the room.

He pictured himself as standing in the farthest corner, where the ceiling sloped down to a narrow, wedgelike space that came within a foot or two of touching the floor. It looked so much cooler over there, away from the rays that slid in through the door and fried narrow portions of Clint's back.

He pictured himself taking up position behind one of the little stacks of crates and barrels along the right side of the cellar. There wasn't much there, but it would have been enough for him to stay out of sight long enough to mount an ambush the next time someone came down to check on him.

Clint's eyes remained fixed on that spot and the previous thought kept echoing through his mind.

When they checked on him.

Whatever little part of Clint's brain that truly entertained that notion dwindled away and died in the space of a couple seconds. Nobody was going to come check on him. There was hardly anyone who even knew he was there at all.

The one or two souls who did know hadn't struck Clint

as the type to get too concerned about Clint's well-being.
Besides, one of those souls was the same one who'd built
the rack that held Clint so sturdily to the underside of that
door. That one person knew damn well that Clint had
better chances of convincing a rat to chew through the
iron rings than of finding some flaw in the thing's design.

There it was again.

Done in by superior craftsmanship.

No matter how much that idea rattled around in his
brain, Clint couldn't get over the irony of it. And no matter how much those rings chewed into his flesh and that
rope threatened to squeeze the life out of him, he couldn't
help but admire the situation he was in.

It took a special kind of mind to come up with a death
like the one in store for Clint Adams. Everything right
down to the angle of the door and the height of the room
itself blended together to form a demise that was as elegant as it was terrible.

Clint could feel the strength going from his legs and
there wasn't a damn thing he could do about it.

He could feel the breath catching in the back of his
throat and all he could do was choke on every last one.

As his muscles tightened and loosened, tightened and
loosened, all he could do was keep the air flowing through
his lungs as best he could and let his mind take him to a
time when the open sky was visible over his head.

FOUR

It wasn't that long ago.

In fact, as far as Clint could tell, it was still only about three days ago that he'd spotted that jagged line of buildings on the eastern horizon. Still taking his time and enjoying his leisurely pace, Clint had steered Eclipse toward those buildings and started wondering if he might want to feel a mattress under his weary body that night or not.

The stars and open sky had their appeal, but so did four walls and a soft pillow. Besides, variety was one of the more enjoyable spices in his life. With that in mind, Clint decided to make his decision at the spur of the moment. He wouldn't know where he'd be sleeping until it was time to close his eyes.

There was a certain charm to that, which appealed to Clint especially after the thoughts that had been drifting around inside of him those last several days. Having that much time to think only allowed Clint to recall such amenities as a hot bath and a close shave. Flicking Eclipse's reins slightly, Clint quickened the stallion's pace and decided to spend the night in a hotel after all. It was going to be a while before he'd make it to the next big town and there was plenty of time to sleep under the stars until then.

Although Clint didn't remember the name of the little town in front of him, he was pretty sure he'd been there at least once before. There wasn't anything particularly interesting about the place that struck his mind as much as its location. All he knew was that there was a clump of buildings in that general vicinity. As he drew closer to the place, he realized immediately why he couldn't remember much else.

Quite simply, there wasn't much else for him to remember.

One of the last towns he'd been to in Kansas was small, but this place before him was downright miniscule. Something about the little collection of run-down buildings made him wonder if they were even really the town he'd been to at all.

He couldn't quite put his finger on it right away, but Clint got a strange feeling in the pit of his stomach the closer he got to the little town. Before too long, he knew exactly what made everything look so strange. There was nobody else around.

Nobody walking the streets.

No horses or wagons pulling into or out of the area.

Not even any voices or any other sounds that came along with more than a handful of people settling in one place. Any other town had footsteps echoing between the buildings, doors slamming shut, hammers pounding on nails or anvils, any number of things that told someone's ears he was nearing civilization. But even as Clint got within a rock's throw of the outer row of buildings, he still had yet to hear a single thing besides the wind or Eclipse's hooves plodding over the ground.

Clint kept his eyes on the place as well. As the strange

silence worked through him, he watched for any sights that might prove his suspicions wrong. But there was only slightly more for him to see than there was to hear. Apart from the buildings themselves, he might as well have kept his eyes shut altogether.

That was what made the place seem smaller. It was so still and so quiet that it resembled a painting of a town rather than any place he could actually visit. By this time, Clint was just riding onto what was probably the main street. There were storefronts and the skeletal remains of a boardwalk, but not much else. A quick look around told him that there were at least two or three other streets branching off from the first one, but he didn't think those would look any different.

Although Clint was a little surprised to find the place so deserted, he wasn't completely taken off guard. He'd seen his fair share of ghost towns. Especially when traveling through Colorado or any other area where mining was a popular draw, abandoned towns were fairly common. A place could empty out faster than it boomed, sometimes, and Clint had even seen stores with merchandise still on its shelves.

Thinking along those lines, Clint felt a familiar itch form at the back of his head. With all the wandering and casual exploring he'd been doing, he found himself in a perfect mood to take a walk through the town and see just how deserted it was. Maybe he could find some explanation as to what had driven so many people out of their homes. Maybe he could find some supplies that had been left behind in a rush.

Clint laughed under his breath and swung down from his saddle. Since there was nobody else around, he decided there was no reason to make up excuses for his own actions. He was curious . . . plain and simple. Besides, there was a saloon up ahead with a trough of water outside its door.

After checking the trough quickly, he saw that it was filled with mostly rainwater but looked clean enough. Eclipse lowered his nose to it, took a tentative taste and then started lapping it up in greedy swallows.

"We're testing all the old sayings today, huh, boy?" Clint said as he patted Eclipse on the neck. "I led you to water. Now we'll see about what curiosity does to this cat."

If the Darley Arabian stallion even heard Clint's words, he was too thirsty to let him know. Situated in the shadow of the building that seemed empty as far as anyone could tell, the trough sent ripples of enjoyment all down the horse's back.

Steeping up to the shell of the saloon, Clint couldn't help but feel like he was getting the short end of that particular stick. Although he would have liked to have some cold refreshment of his own, he smirked at the use of yet another tried and true saying in just under five minutes.

The double doors leading into the saloon were hanging open. One of them was just about to fall off its hinges as Clint pushed it aside just enough for him to step through. The sound of metal grating against metal wasn't as loud as he might have expected from a ghost town. In fact, it wasn't as much as he would have expected from a door that was still in everyday use.

His footsteps were loud enough to echo through the place, however, and Clint made his way toward a bar that was made up of solid yet poorly constructed timber. The light shone through dirty windows and hit a few stray glasses that were scattered along the top of the bar, creating glimmering reflections when Clint turned his head just the right way.

He stood there looking at those glasses for a moment

or two, studying the way the light shone through them. What kept him staring was one simple fact: Those glasses weren't just the cleanest things in the room. They were spotless.

FIVE

The sight of those clean glasses was the only light inside the cellar that had been so expertly crafted into Clint's prison. It shone in his mind like a beacon, reminding him of just how stupid any man could be.

His muscles tensed and relaxed, strained and let go, as he gritted his teeth and tried not to think about the dryness that was turning his throat into a parched strip of bloody cracks. The heat wasn't as bad as it could have been, but it was enough to make the air thick and almost too heavy to breathe.

It didn't make matters any better as Clint started to slip into thoughts that were harder on him than the restraints secured around his neck and wrists. With a little effort, the tension within his own brain began to ease off a bit.

With a lot *more* effort, he actually started to feel some relief.

It would have been only too easy to be consumed with blaming himself for what had happened or for criticizing himself for the way things had played out. That wasn't the best or brightest way to go, but it was certainly the easiest thing he could have done at that moment. Even

18

so, Clint forced himself to push through what was easiest
and focus on what was necessary.

The cellar was filled with the sounds of Clint's tense,
labored breathing and the creaking of his restraints being
tested over and over again. Jolts of pain lanced through
his wrists and neck, but he used those as a way to keep
himself alert and awake.

His legs were going numb again, so he started slowly
moving them in place. Even flexing his toes inside his
boots seemed to help a little bit and every little bit of help
was sorely appreciated.

Just as he was about to drift away into his thoughts
once again, Clint heard something moving around over
his head. Every muscle froze inside of him and his senses
perked up so much that he could almost hear the blood
pumping through his veins.

Clint could feel something on his back. It wasn't
much; just a few impacts that he could detect through the
cellar door. In fact, it was the only time he was thankful
for the apparatus holding him in place because the rings
and rope amplified the sensations just enough for him to
feel them.

The little tremors were traveling through the ground in
a steady pattern. They grew in intensity as they got closer,
assuring Clint that they were exactly what he thought they
might be.

Footsteps.

Someone was headed toward the cellar and they were
taking their sweet time in getting there. After all, why
hurry when they knew damn well that the man they were
visiting had no chance of moving from his spot?

Clint pictured the smug look that was surely on the
other person's face. Unlike the other thoughts that had
stoked the fires of his anger earlier, he found these images

to do him a world of good. They allowed him to pull up some more strength from his reserves and discover a few other sources besides.

The footsteps stopped so close that Clint thought the unseen person might be standing right on top of him. In fact, judging by the design of the restraints, that person might actually enjoy doing just that for a moment or two. Clint had no trouble at all picturing that bastard standing on the other side of that door with his feet pressing down less than a few inches away from his own shoulder blades.

Clint even concentrated on those same images, forming them in his brain until he felt no more pain in his body and no more fatigue in his muscles. All he felt was the fire building inside of him until he damn near thought he could tear himself free from the restraints altogether.

"How you doin' down there?" came a voice that Clint had only heard a couple times before. "Still breathin', or do I need to come down there and clean up a body?"

Not one sound came out of Clint's mouth. Not one damn sound.

There was more silence for a moment . . . followed by the sound of shifting feet directly over Clint's head.

Clint could feel those feet along his back, as if there was a boot gliding between his outstretched arms. Suddenly, the door above him slammed inward and a jarring crash filled every inch of the cellar. Dust and dirt fell down from between the boards and a splitting pain shot through Clint's aching body.

The door didn't give in, however. Whoever was on the other side had merely pounded his boot against it as a way of letting Clint know he was still there.

"I think I'll give you a little more time to stew," the voice said. "I'll be back with a shovel to pull yer carcass out of there."

Clint nodded slowly as he felt the steps head away. A smirk drifted across his face as he resumed his routine. Muscles flexing and relaxing, testing and easing off. The fire inside him grew.

SIX

When Clint had first stepped into that saloon, he stared at the clean glasses sitting on the bar for a good couple of seconds. His arm tensed slightly as his hand lowered toward his Colt, but he wasn't about to draw just yet. The motion was merely his natural instinct and he barely even noticed that it had happened.

Clint walked into the saloon and up to the bar, looking and listening for any sign of life besides his own within the place. He made it all the way across the room, past several overturned tables and chairs, and up to the bar without hearing a single thing to give him pause.

In fact, standing in front of the bar, Clint was starting to feel a little foolish for letting something so simple get on his nerves like that. He reached out and picked up one of the glasses, holding it up to the light so he could get a better look.

In the space of an instant, the warning sensation in his mind came flooding back to him. The glass he'd picked up wasn't completely clean, after all. There was still a couple of drops of brownish liquid collected in the bottom.

More of a beer drinker himself, Clint still had no problem identifying the smell of whiskey when he lifted the glass to his nose and took a whiff. Even his limited knowledge on the subject was enough to tell him that the liquor wasn't the best around, but the fact that there was any at all in the glass told him plenty.

Mainly, it told him that the town wasn't nearly as deserted as it appeared.

As if responding to the thought that was still fresh in his mind, a sound rumbled through the saloon, coming from the back of the room. Clint slapped the glass down onto the bar and turned on the balls of his feet toward the noise. When he did, he immediately spotted a figure standing in a battered doorway next to a stage that was just big enough for a pair of dancers at the most.

"Take it easy there, friend," the other man said as he lifted his hands and put on a shaky grin. "I didn't mean to startle you."

Although Clint had yet to draw his weapon, he kept his hand poised an inch or so over the Colt's handle.

The other man looked to be in his late thirties, with every year of his life leaving its mark in deep grooves along his face and neck. He had the kind of skin that looked as though it had been left tacked to the side of a barn for a few years in the blazing sun before being slapped onto his skull. Even so, the smile he wore seemed genuine enough and he didn't appear to be wearing a weapon.

The man wore simple, if not worn-out, clothes and had his shirtsleeves rolled up past his elbows. His faded jeans sported more than a couple holes and a few hastily placed patches that were only slightly stronger than the flaws they covered. Broad shoulders would have made his head look a little small if not for the bushy sideburns that flowed all the way down to the corners of his mouth.

"If yer thirsty, I can fix ya somethin'," the man said. "I would'a been here sooner, but I'm sure you can see that business ain't exactly been too good lately."

Clint relaxed a bit and walked up to the other man. "You can put your hands down. I'm not going to hurt you."

Relief washed over the man's face and he let out a deep breath. "Glad to hear it. A man can never be too sure around here. There's been plenty of no-good types who come through here looting or setting fires just because there ain't nobody around to stop 'em."

"You're around," Clint pointed out.

Shrugging, the man said, "Yeah, but I'm not the type to stop them kind of types. It just ain't worth it."

"So what happened here? I came through here not too long ago and this was a nice enough town. Where is everyone?"

Feeling a little more at ease, the other man stepped up to the bar and rubbed the palms of his hands over its dusty surface. "There's no tellin' where they went."

"Are you saying they just disappeared?"

The man slowly craned his neck and fixed his eyes on Clint, letting a moment or two slip by without saying a word. There was something in the fellow's eyes that didn't quite fit. Then again, in a town that was empty for all but one man, there wasn't a whole lot that *would have* fit.

Clint wasn't sure if the man was trying to make him feel uncomfortable or if he was just trying to think of what he should say next. Whatever the reason for his silence, the guy held it long enough for Clint to start to get suspicious. Suddenly, the man's eyes went wide and his lips curled up into a sloppy smile.

"Yeah," he said. "They all disappeared. Just like a bunch'a ghosts!" He couldn't say much more before breaking out into laughter that filled up the empty room and nearly shook the dust off the rafters.

Although Clint still didn't know quite what to make of

him, he found himself laughing as well. The whole situation just seemed so odd that he couldn't help himself. Finally, after both men had gotten it out of their systems, they caught their breath and sized each other up.

"The name's Morgan," the man said as he stuck out a leathery hand and grinned.

"I'm Clint," he said, grasping the other's hand and shaking it. "So what happened to everyone in town?"

"They're gone."

"I could tell that much on my own. Where did they go?"

Morgan shrugged. "Who knows? Once things started drying up around here, they found greener pastures, I guess."

"So this was a boomtown?"

Once again, Morgan shrugged. Clint didn't need any of his skills at reading people to know that the other man just didn't want to talk about what had cleared out the streets and buildings of the town. Since he wasn't about to make it his mission to find out, Clint decided to let the subject rest.

Nodding toward the whiskey glass, Clint asked, "Any beer left around here?"

"How should I know?"

"Isn't that your drink?"

"No," Morgan said as a shadow fell over Clint's back. "It's his."

The *click* of a pistol hammer snapping back rattled through the saloon like a shot echoing in the walls of a barren canyon.

SEVEN

Whoever had come up behind Clint had done so with more stealth than a cat sneaking across a carpeted floor. The only warning Clint got before he knew it was too late was the shadow growing on the bar next to his own. Seeing that without hearing a damn thing made Clint think the shadow was being thrown by something outside the saloon's window. Only the sound of the gun being cocked proved him wrong.

If his reflexes had taken over a fraction of a second later . . . he would have been *dead* wrong.

Spinning on the balls of his feet, Clint twisted around so that he could look at who was behind him. He kept Morgan in the corner of his eye just in case the man at the bar decided to try to take advantage of the new arrival's distraction.

The sun was beaming through the window as well as the open door, making it impossible for Clint to see anything more than a hazy outline at first. He might not have been able to tell if the guy was smiling or frowning, but he could see the gun in the man's hand and that was all that mattered. The fact that the other gun had already been cocked was on Clint's mind as he held his fire for a second and jumped to one side, away from where Morgan was standing.

The shot went off, sending a round through the musty air until it slammed into the edge of the bar. Splinters peeled away from the wood and showered down onto the floor. The debris didn't even get a chance to settle before another shot blew away the silence.

In the blink of an eye, Clint had plucked the Colt from its spot at his side and had pulled his trigger. He fired from the hip, using his instincts more than his eyesight to guide his shot. The pistol bucked against his hand a split-second before the shadowy figure at the door was knocked off his feet.

Clint wheeled around to glare at Morgan, ready to react in case the other man still wanted to try something. But not only was Morgan not aiming a gun at him, he wasn't anywhere to be seen. Clint didn't have too long to ponder the other man's whereabouts since the once-silent saloon had erupted into sudden chaos.

All attempts at sneaking around were shoved to the wayside and boots pounded against the floorboards in a rush to get into the room. The sounds seemed to come from all sides as men started pouring in from the front door as well as back rooms and a few other doors that Clint hadn't even noticed before they were opened.

After taking a quick look around, Clint spotted at least four more armed men rushing into the saloon's main room. They opened fire the instant they got him in their sights, filling the air with a fiery swarm of lead.

Clint knew the first thing he needed was some cover. And since there wasn't much else in the room that wasn't knocked over or falling apart, he put one hand flat upon the bar and used it to hoist himself up and over the wooden structure.

The bar might not have been a picture of fine crafts-manship, but the planks were sturdy enough to stop a few of the rounds that came screaming in his direction. More importantly, it took him out of sight before one of the gunmen got in a lucky shot.

As soon as his boots hit the floor, Clint dropped down into a low crouch and waited for the first round of firing to taper off. A few more holes were punched through the wood on either side of him as the shooters decided to find a target before starting in again.

Once the roar of the gunshots drifted away, that same silence fell upon the place as when Clint had first walked through the saloon's doors. If he concentrated, Clint could hear the hint of a boot scraping against the floor, but not much else. Another old phrase sprung to mind: quiet as a tomb. No matter how much it fit the situation, Clint pushed it out of his thoughts.

Without moving his feet, Clint leaned to one side so he could take a peek through a freshly-made bullet hole. He couldn't see any of the gunmen, but he wasn't exactly looking for them in the first place. What he searched for was the same thing that had tipped him off to the first one's presence a minute ago.

After peering through the crude circle, he managed to catch sight of exactly what he'd been looking for: shadows.

The black outlines moved across the floor even faster than Clint had been expecting. Even though he'd witnessed the men's stealth firsthand, he still could hardly believe just how quickly they could move without making more than a hint of sound.

While the others might have known how to sneak, they still weren't fast enough to get the drop on their prey. By the time they'd closed in around the bar, Clint had positioned himself where he wanted to be and was ready to make his move.

He'd gotten himself a few more feet toward the back end of the bar while doing a decent job of keeping himself quiet. Apparently, the men considered their light steps to be their main advantage and pressed it to its fullest. But now that Clint had seen it for himself, he wasn't about to let even a cat sneak up on him again.

Like a train switching onto an alternate track, Clint switched his mind over to focus onto an alternate sense. He paid less attention to what his ears were (or weren't) telling him and more to what he could see or feel. The shadows were still moving; there was nothing anyone could do about that. When they walked, the gunmen's boots still made an impact upon the ground. Even without sound, Clint could still feel those steps through the soles of his own boots if he concentrated hard enough.

He didn't get much, but he got a better idea of where the shooters were coming from than if he kept trying to listen for sounds that simply weren't there. With a vague picture in his mind about what was waiting for him on the other side of the bar, Clint steeled himself and got ready to break from cover.

All he could do was hope that his senses hadn't painted the wrong picture.

EIGHT

Using every sense but his hearing, Clint felt as though the world had slowed down a notch as he moved forward and raised up to stand behind the bar. He took in everything around him, which made it all the stranger that he felt as though he'd gone deaf through sheer force of will.

It wasn't that he couldn't hear anything, but he just didn't allow himself to hear. After all, the only thing for him to hear as he broke out from where he'd been crouching was the thunderous roar of gunfire, which turned the air into a storm of violence.

Clint felt the bullets whip past him and raised his Colt to take aim on the first man's outline he could see. There was a figure standing less than five feet away from him and had been about two steps from charging around the bar toward where Clint had been hiding.

The gunman held on to a .38 revolver as though it was the source of life itself. Adjusting his aim slightly to point the weapon at Clint while continuing to move on his own, the gunman squeezed his trigger and flinched as another shot blasted through the air in front of him. The only reason that particular shot surprised him, however, was because it didn't come from his own weapon.

Even with every last element working against him, Clint had still managed to move and fire before the other man could get an aimed shot off. Not only that, but he'd put his round exactly on the spot where his eyes were looking.

The Colt spat its bullet somewhere just below the gunman's collarbone, hitting with enough impact to send the recipient flying backward and slamming against the floor. He landed with a solid *thump*, both legs clattering against the floor in a final spasm as his gun dropped out of his hands.

The moment Clint saw that he'd put his target down, he turned his sights toward the next one. There would be plenty of time to go back and tie up any loose ends once those same ends were no longer throwing live ammunition in his direction.

Shots were still flying through the air all around him as he turned toward the second set of footfalls Clint had felt a couple seconds earlier. Sure enough, his senses proved right again and pointed him toward a bulky man dressed in a frayed jacket with a face covered in streaks of grime.

This one had a pistol in each fist. He took a shot with the left gun while starting to pull the trigger on the right. His dirty features were twisted in the ugly mixture of tense expectation and fear that marked the faces of many men when they fired their guns at another living person.

Clint could tell just by looking at him that the man was not a gunfighter. On the other hand, that didn't mean that the guy wasn't dangerous. Anyone pointing a gun at him was considered dangerous. The only thing Clint had to decide was how he should deal with that particular danger.

Of course, he only had about half a second to make that decision.

In less time than that, Clint adjusted his aim and pulled his trigger, blowing a hole through the gunman's thigh.

Without stopping to watch as the man spun around in a
tight circle and keeled over, Clint looked toward the next
man, who was at the far end of the bar.

Although he'd been able to drop the first two without
much problem, even Clint Adams wasn't fast enough to
move and put down another so easily. His mind was
working at full steam, already picturing where he would
have to fire next. Before he could take the shot, however,
the man at the other end of the bar took one of his own.

The shotgun blast was unmistakable. It dwarfed the
other gunshots the way a stick of dynamite dwarfed a
firecracker. A plume of smoke rolled from both barrels
and the hailstorm of lead wasn't far behind.

Clint's reflexes took command of the rest of him, pitch-
ing him down to the floor as quickly as possible. Hoping
for scattershot as opposed to some kind of heavier ammunition, Clint winced with the knowledge that he would
find out what the gun was loaded with before he hit the
ground. If it was scattershot, the bar would probably ab-
sorb a good deal of the damage. As far as the other alter-
native . . . well . . . Clint had heard of some men loading
nickels and dimes into shotgun shells, which could nearly
cut a full-grown mule into two pieces. Against that, the
bar wouldn't be much cover at all.

The drop to the floor seemed to take forever. All the
while, Clint knew that he could be feeling lead tearing
through his flesh at any second. The first thing he felt was
a burning sting on his shoulders, quickly followed by
stabbing pains in his back and neck. Actually, the pain
felt more like rusty blades slicing through his skin, twisting a bit before coming out again.

Clint's chest and left arm hit the floor at the same time,
sending his body into a roll that took him the rest of the
way beneath the bar. Looking up and around, he saw a
chunk of the bar had been taken out over his head, but it
was a messy piece of work. It looked as though some of

the wood had been chipped and peeled back by a crowbar.

After checking the bloody sections of his own body, Clint let out a sigh of relief. It had been scattershot after all. Larger ammunition would have blown a bigger hole in the bar and would have taken off his arm if it had hit him in the same places as he'd been hit. Unfortunately, that didn't make the wounds hurt any less.

By this time, the room was beginning to fill up with more sounds than just the gunshots. The footsteps were getting louder and the man with the two guns was thrashing about on the floor, spewing a stream of obscenities as the pain from his wound really started to kick in. But Clint didn't rely on that for anything, since too much noise was just as bad as not enough. He didn't need to hear those things by that time, anyway. The shotgunner hadn't had enough time to move from the last place Clint had seen him.

Still keeping his body flat against the ground, Clint pointed the Colt at the bar and imagined the wooden structure wasn't even there. One flicker of a shadow was all he needed to see before he pulled his trigger twice in quick succession.

The first shot knocked a hole through the bar and the second went through a hole that was already there. As soon as the bullets had been spent, Clint's hands flew into motion as he quickly reloaded his weapon.

As his fingers emptied his cylinder, Clint watched and felt for any sign that someone was coming his way. He'd already taken fresh rounds from his gun belt and started sliding them into the Colt when he heard and felt the thump of something heavy hitting the floorboards. Peeking through one of the bullet holes, Clint saw the shotgunner on his knees as the blank stare of death drifted onto his face.

From what he could see, Clint had hit the other man with both shots. One hit the shotgunner in the stomach and the other took a chunk from his arm, which now dangled at his side like a broken branch hanging from a tree.

Clint kept his eyes on that man until the shotgunner finally toppled forward onto his face. He was still groaning and moving, but wasn't about to do much else for a while . . . if ever.

After getting his feet beneath him, Clint kept himself low while waiting for any other sign that the shooting was about to start again. The Colt was fully loaded and his finger was on the trigger, one thought away from firing another shot.

The saloon was quiet. Not only that, but Clint couldn't feel any motion on the floor or see anything bigger than dust particles moving through the air. He knew there was at least one or two men out there, but was sick and tired of letting them sneak around behind his back. Then again, he knew better than to stand straight up and give them a perfect target.

Just then, his eyes drifted down to the bar. As he'd noticed before, the wood was sturdy enough, but wasn't put together too well. Suddenly, that didn't seem like such a bad thing.

NINE

There were two men left in the saloon. One of them had busted in with the other three when they got the signal to attack. The second had come in after the shooting started as backup in case some was needed. Judging by the fact that three men were on the floor and two were obviously dead, backup was most definitely needed.

The man who'd been there since the first shots were fired motioned with his hand to where he knew Clint was hiding. After getting a nod from the other man in response, he walked slowly toward the bar, holding his gun at the ready. Every step he took was careful and deliberate, landing with the ball of his foot first, before allowing his weight to settle into the step.

He winced as he heard the slightest of squeaks coming from beneath his boot, but kept on moving anyway. Just to be careful, he changed direction slightly on the off chance that Clint might have heard the little slip.

Focusing his senses on the area in front of him, the man could hear some movement behind the bar. In the stillness of the deserted saloon, the muted shuffle of feet against the floor might as well have been a voice shouting to be heard. His grip tightening around the handle of his

gun, the man let himself breathe a little easier, comfortable in the knowledge that he could once again get the
drop on his target.

He flinched when he heard a loud *thump* come from
the other side of the bar. It wasn't the sound of someone's
feet pounding against the floor, or even a body toppling
over. Instead, it sounded more like something bashing
against the bar itself.

The gunman froze where he was and held up a warning
hand, knowing that his partner behind him would see and
understand the signal. Raising his weapon and taking aim,
the gunman used his other hand to signal for the man
behind him to make his way around the bar on the other
side. He didn't have to see or hear anything to be sure
that the other man was following orders.

Secure that he still had surprise and numbers on his
side, the gunman started to step forward yet again when
he was stopped by another loud bashing sound. This time,
the noise was tainted with a crunch and was quickly followed by another slam. Before he could figure out what
was happening, the bottom section of the front of the bar
splintered apart as a section of wooden planks was kicked
out.

Once the wooden planks gave way beneath his foot,
Clint rolled against the side of the bar and smashed down
the panels with his shoulder. After having been shot up
and battered, the side of the bar gave way rather easily as
Clint pushed his body through with no intention of being
stopped.

In fact, as soon as the side of the bar gave way, the top
started to shift and creak like an animal with three broken
legs. Rolling through the hole he'd just created, Clint
sighted down the Colt's barrel and squeezed off a shot.
The pistol bucked in his hand and delivered its cargo
straight into the closest man's midsection.

Still rolling, Clint took another shot, which caught his

target squarely in the heart. From the angle where Clint was firing, the impact of the bullet lifted the gunman slightly off his feet and knocked him back a couple steps. Once that man was out of the way, Clint steered himself for one of the overturned tables that he just happened to spot from the corner of his eye.

The once-quiet saloon was again roaring with noise. This time, instead of just the gunfire and heavy steps, there was the rumble of wood caving in on itself as the bar toppled in on itself like a mine caving in. Clint's opinions about the shoddy way the bar had been built was confirmed as the entire thing collapsed amid a flood of dust and splinters.

Coming to a stop once his ribs bumped up against the table leg, Clint craned his neck for a look around the room. He held the Colt in front of him, sighting down its barrel and preparing to fire at a moment's notice. For a minute, it was hard to see much of anything with all the gritty debris settling around him. Little bits of wood and dirt stung his nostrils with every breath as Clint struggled to keep his eyes open through the gritty curtain, which lowered to the floor.

Another shot went off, pulling Clint's eyes toward its source, but all he could see was the man he'd just shot clutching his chest with one hand while gasping for breath. That one still held on to his pistol. In fact, it looked as though his twitching finger was what had caused that last gunshot to be fired.

Without taking his eyes away from his search, Clint scrambled to get to his feet. He reached out with his free hand and pulled the table over toward him. The tabletop was round, so it didn't take much to wheel it between himself and the front door. Once that was done, he crouched behind it and waited.

It wouldn't have taken a cat to sneak up on him in those following seconds. The gunshots were still ringing in

Clint's ears and the blood was pumping through him so quickly that it filled his skull with a deafening rush that reminded him of a waterfall.

But he wasn't just using his sense of hearing. In fact, Clint had gotten to the point where he'd seen enough of the saloon's interior to have a good idea of the layout in his mind. He checked a couple key locations over and over again, alert for the next attack that could come at any second.

Working his way around the table, Clint scanned the entire room before he straightened up and stood tall. The little gouges in his back stung like hell, but they weren't much to concern himself about. He knew they had to be cleaned and might need a stitch or two, but that was about it. He used the sharp pain to heighten the rest of his senses as he made his way through the room and toward the front door.

Smoke still hung heavily in the air and one of the men was shifting slightly in place, but those were the only signs of movement he could see. Clint thought there had been one other gunman in the room, but couldn't see hide nor hair of him anymore.

After glancing down at the faces he could see, Clint kept his gun at the ready and walked to the front of the room. He turned on his heels and let his eyes wander. From his new vantage, Clint could see parts of the saloon that he hadn't been able to before. Most important, he saw a door that he'd missed when he'd first walked inside.

Clint moved away from the front doorway and walked over to the one gunman who was still moving. That one was crumpled on the floor, gritting his teeth against the waves of pain that coursed through his body.

"All right," Clint said as he looked down at the wounded man. "I want to know how many of you there are and where the rest have gone to."

"I-I'll bet you do."

Without even moving his hand that held the Colt, Clint nodded slowly and spoke in a low, menacing voice. "I want to know those things . . . and you're going to tell them to me."

"F-fu—"

Before the rest of that word could come out of the gunman's mouth, Clint moved his foot outward and placed the tip of his toe on the open wound in the other man's leg. With the slightest bit of pressure, he pushed down and then let his toe up.

"You might want to reconsider what you're about to say," Clint said without moving his boot away from the bloody bullet hole. "You're hurt, but not nearly bad enough to take you away from here before I get to spend some time with you."

This time, when the gunman looked up, his eyes weren't quite as indignant as they'd been before.

TEN

Clint was just about to fall asleep as the memories of the fight in the saloon made their way through his mind. The gunshots still echoed as they had those days ago and the smell of dust and gunpowder still seemed fresh in his nose. Although his blood stirred within him like it had before, it wasn't enough to fight back the fatigue that pressed down on him like a lead weight balanced on his shoulders.

His body still went through its motions, straining and relaxing while testing the strength of his restraints. He stopped when he heard the distinctive sound of footsteps returning. Clint's mind was drawing close to the point where he was having a hard time distinguishing what his different senses were telling him.

Did he hear those footsteps or feel them on his back?

Did he see a shadow eclipsing the fading sunlight filtering down onto him or were his eyes just starting to give out like candles that had reached the end of their wicks?

At that point in time, Clint didn't even care what those answers were. All he knew was that someone was coming.

And if he felt that bastard's boot slamming down on the other side of the door, he'd be liable to—

Slam.

The fire inside Clint Adams roared with a life of its own and his jaw became set in a grim mask. Clenching fists at the ends of both arms, he stared straight ahead and tried not to give the man at the other side of that door what he was after.

"You still down there?" came the tormenting voice. "I got the shovel with me this time, so I might as well pay you a visit to see for myself."

With that, the footsteps faded away and the clatter of a couple doors could be heard. Clint had only heard those doors once before, but the sound of them was something he'd been waiting for ever since. Hearing those doors meant that the only other way out of the cellar besides the door he was hanging from was being opened. And if the way was opened, that made it all the more easier for him to get out.

At least . . . it was easier in theory. The restraints keeping Clint in place were still strong. However, there had been a promising squeak accompanying the last several flexes of Clint's arms and neck.

He could feel the steps as their impact traveled through the ground and into the walls of the cellar. From there, the vibrations went through the wooden door and finally into the device strangling the life from Clint's body one drop at a time.

Although he couldn't see the door itself, Clint couldn't miss the opening that formed in the wall to his left. Something swung inward and a familiar figure stepped inside. As promised, he carried a shovel over one shoulder.

The figure was lean and wiry, moving with the skittish speed and stooped posture of a rat. His frame was so bony in places that it seemed a wonder that he could support the weight of the shovel on his back without letting the tool drop to the ground in exhaustion. The man's eyes reflected anything but pain, however. His mouth curled into an ugly grin.

"You still in there?" the man asked, peering into Clint's eyes.

Clint didn't blink. He didn't even move until he let out a quick breath and spat into the rat-man's face.

Rather than get upset by the juicy insult, Rat-man lifted his free hand and wiped the spittle from his cheek. Smiling, he rubbed his thumb and forefinger together as if somehow studying Clint's saliva. "If I was you, I would've kept more of my water to myself. Especially since you won't be gettin' any from me or anyone else."

"Don't say that," Clint said sarcastically. "You're liable to disappoint me."

Suddenly, the rat-man hefted his shovel with both hands and cocked it back over his shoulder as though he was about to take a massive swing at Clint's skull. He stayed in position while putting on a fierce, crooked sneer.

Seeing what the other man was about to do, Clint leaned his head forward until the rope bit into his throat. This time, like all the others, he used the pain to fuel his effort and keep his vision from blacking out along the edges.

Clint locked eyes with the rat-man and stared with an intensity that was felt all the way through to the back of the smaller man's head. "Go ahead, you little prick," Clint said in a voice that was a rumbling snarl in the shadows. "If you're going to take your shot, you'd better make it a good one because when I'm out of here, I'll push that shovel so far down your throat, you'll be shitting splinters for the rest of your life."

The rat-man did his level best to keep up the bad look he'd put on. But as Clint's words and powerful glare sunk in, he couldn't come up with another threat to fire back. In fact, the shovel even started to waver slightly in his grasp. Rather than let it drop from his hands altogether, he set the head of the shovel down and leaned against the handle.

"Maybe I'll wait here and watch you die," the skinny man said. "It shouldn't take too much longer."

"Maybe you'll want to fetch your master so he can watch it, too?"

When he didn't get a reply, Clint asked, "Where's Morgan? I thought he'd be the one to come by and talk tough while I was all trussed up like this."

"Morgan?" Rat-man seemed genuinely perplexed that that name would even come up in conversation. "Who's that?"

Suddenly, the skinny man with the shovel shook off whatever interest he'd had in the conversation. "Only question you should have is how long before you die." That seemed to amuse him to no end and the corners of his mouth turned up as if they were attached to fishhooks.

"What about Paula?" Clint asked. "She around, too?"

The expression on Rat-man's face turned somewhat wistful as he nodded slowly. "But she don't want to see you," he answered with a little too much venom in his tone. "You just forget about her!"

Clint eased back against his restraints and nodded. Figuring out the skinny runt's pressure points was too easy. All he had to do now was wait for a good moment to squeeze.

ELEVEN

Even when he was running, Morgan hardly made a sound. After the gunfight in the saloon, he'd bolted through the cramped confines of a corridor so narrow that even the daylight had a hard time breaking in. But Morgan didn't have to see where he was going to know where to turn or when to slow down and hop down or up a couple stairs. He knew those corridors like the back of his own hand. In fact he was the only one left who knew *all* of them.

When he came to the end of that particular corridor, he turned his face away from the bright outline that marked the spot where the door panel fit into a wall. He slowed only slightly while reaching out with one hand to press against the spot where a doorknob should have been.

There was no handle, but there was a small section on the door that moved in slightly at the proper touch. It wasn't a complex mechanism, but the trigger was molded so well into the rest of the door that it would have taken careful examination for someone to figure out that it was even there. When pressed, it activated a lever that allowed the door to swing open with the weakest push.

Morgan emerged from the darkness and stepped into a small office filled with bookcases, a chest of drawers, a

small table and a rack filled with guns of all shapes and
sizes. Besides the pistols, rifles and shotguns, there were
a few knives, a bayonet and a woodcutting ax. Although
his eyes went immediately to the weapons hanging on the
rack, he didn't reach out for a single one of them. Instead,
he shut the door behind him, dropped to a sitting position
on the floor and leaned against the empty wall.

There was no trace of the door. All that could be seen
was the wall, which blended in perfectly with all the other
walls, right down to the dirt streaks, water stains and occasional cracks. Morgan pressed the palms of his hands
against his face, clenched his eyes shut and let out an
exasperated gasp that filled the room with a sound similar
to steam hissing from a train's engine.

"How could this happen? How could this happen?"
Morgan said to himself while rocking back and forth.
"Why did this have to happen? Why here? Why now?"

Suddenly, he stopped talking and snapped his hands
away from his face. The words were cut off so quickly
that his mouth was frozen in the process of forming another sentence. His eyes widened and darted from side to
side as his breath remained wedged in the back of his
throat.

Morgan twisted his head to one side with such speed
that a few wet pops came from the joints in his neck.
Slowly, he leaned back until his head and shoulders were
both pressed tightly against the door. He closed his eyes
and muttered to himself without making a sound. His lips
merely moved to form words that didn't have any breath
behind them.

When he moved away from the wall, he did so with
such care that it looked as if he was peeling himself away
after being glued into place. Once he was free of the wall,
he crawled forward a step or two and jumped to his feet.
From there, he reached out to the weapon rack, took hold

of the first thing he could grab and wheeled around to face the wall.

The first thing he could grab was the woodcutting ax and he held it in both hands, ready to bury its blade into whoever had emerged from the secret door. Once the ax was cocked over one shoulder, Morgan froze in that position and waited. His eyes were wide and fixed on the hidden panel in the wall.

Within a few seconds, a scraping could be heard behind that wall. It sounded like teeth and claws of some very big vermin as hands searched in the dark for the panel to open the door. Finally, the person on the other side managed to press the right spot and the door swung away from the wall. Morgan stayed right where he was, preparing to swing his ax as all the muscles in his arms tensed with anticipation.

Emerging from the shadows of the narrow corridor, hurrying through as if something was pushing from the other side, a slender figure stepped into the room and immediately closed the door. The figure dusted off its shoulders and then pulled back a hood attached to the back of a thin cloak. Once the hood was gone, the figure revealed herself to be a thin woman with thick brown hair that fell down several inches past her shoulders.

She had a little bow-shaped mouth and high cheekbones. The most impressive part of her face, however, was her large chocolate brown eyes. They weren't abnormally large, but only seemed big because they were so finely shaped and almost eerily captivating.

Revealing a dark brown dress once she removed the cloak, she shook the outer garment a couple times to get some of the dust off that had fallen onto her during her walk through the dark. Her skirt slit up along one side to a spot slightly higher than her knee. Through the cut in the fabric, a small holster could be seen strapped to her thigh.

"What are you doing here?" Morgan asked. He still had the ax hefted over one shoulder and looked as though he might just try to bury it into the brunette soon enough.

"I'm supposed to meet him here," she said impatiently. Although she'd seen the crude weapon in Morgan's hand, the brunette didn't really seem to care about it.

"Meet who here?"

"Who do you think? Alonzo. This *is* his office, isn't it?"

Morgan thought about that for a second before letting out the breath he'd been holding and lowering the ax. "Yeah. This is his office." Once he'd pulled himself together a bit more, he asked, "Were you followed?"

The brunette didn't even try to hide the annoyance she felt when looking at the other man. Despite the fact that Morgan was a couple inches taller than she, the brunette carried herself as if she towered over him. "Of course I wasn't followed," she spat back. "I know what I'm doing."

"Well, then you should know that Alonzo wouldn't want you around here. Not with all that shooting going on and that intruder coming into his town. Mr. Mason would want you to meet him somewhere else. Try his other office."

"Intruder? It's only one man. He's taken care of more intruders than that without any trouble."

"Not one like this one," Morgan replied while shrinking away from the brunette like a dog that had been whipped too many times. "This one's trouble. Trouble of a sort we ain't never seen before."

Stepping over to the table, she lifted her leg and set it on the edge of the wooden surface. From there, she removed the derringer from the holster at her thigh and checked to make sure it was loaded. "Then maybe we'll have to give him some special treatment."

TWELVE

Clint wasn't the kind of man given to torturing another for information. After the smoke had cleared at the saloon, leaving Clint alone with one of the wounded men who'd been shooting at him moments before, he did find himself in a good situation to create some false impressions. Clint knew he wasn't about to hurt anyone more than he had to for any reason. But that didn't mean that anyone else had to know that.

The wounded gunman had talked a tough game, but in the end his own imagination got the best of him. Of course, Clint knew what to say to stoke the fires beneath that same imagination as well. In the end, Clint found out what he needed to know and he hadn't even had to do anything more than ask one or two more times . . . with his boot poised over the other man's wound.

It turned out that the town he'd entered had been renamed since the last time he'd paid it a visit. It had used to be called West Bend, but now it was known as Mason. And, according to the gunman, it was named after the man who'd proclaimed himself sole ruler of the town after it had been deserted.

Alonzo Mason was that man's name and he seemed to

have spotted some kind of golden opportunity once most of the residents of West Bend had decided to pick up and leave once the wells dried up and a major cattle company started taking another route for their drives. According to that gunman, all of that had happened just over a year ago and Mason jumped right in to keep hold of the place that he called home.

So the town wasn't quite as deserted as Clint had thought. In fact, once the gunman had started talking, all Clint had to do was sit back and listen to the words that came spilling out of his mouth. One of the other things the man told him was that a group of people who didn't have enough money to pull up their stakes and leave town had decided to stick around and live Alonzo Mason's way.

Of course, that way was enforced by men like the ones who had come into the saloon shooting the place full of holes. After that, Clint was hearing a lot of other talk that began to be infused with more threats than information. At that point, he'd started to leave the saloon and head out through the front door.

"Hold on," the gunman said. "You ain't just gonna leave me here, are ya?"

Clint stood in the doorway and looked over his shoulder. "That was the idea."

"But you promised—"

"I promised I wouldn't hurt you," Clint said sharply. "I'm no doctor, so I can't exactly help you too much in that respect."

"But I'm hurt." The gunman winced and choked back an agonized groan. Whether or not that was coming from actual pain or dramatics was hard to tell. Either way, he somehow found the strength to speak before too long. "I'll die if you leave me here. I'm bleedin'."

Clint shrugged. "If we would've met under more sociable circumstances, that might have concerned me a little more. If you want sympathy, I guess you're asking the wrong man." With that, Clint pushed the door open and stepped outside. In his mind, he was counting down the seconds. Before he could reach zero in his thoughts, he heard the gunman's voice shouting out from behind him.

"Wait," the wounded man said in a tone that no longer had exaggerated pain in it. This time, he sounded truly desperate. "I'll tell you what you wanted to know."

Clint stopped. He'd had no intention of leaving that man. Not yet, anyway. It was his turn to lay on some dramatics and he did so with just enough flair to make his act seem convincing. After waiting a couple of seconds, he turned around and stared at the man laying on the floor. "I thought you already told me everything."

"I told you some . . . but . . . not everything."

"So you were lying to me?" Clint asked, pouring on his anger a little thicker to try and save some time.

It worked.

"No!" the gunman shouted. "I didn't lie. I just . . . didn't tell you everything."

"So start talking."

The gunman swallowed hard and looked up at Clint with a set of eyes that would have made a puppy shake its head with admiration. Wanting to step on the other man's bloody wound more than ever, Clint fought back the impulse and went over to him.

"What do you want?" Clint asked.

"Something to drink. To take the edge off."

Clint walked toward the bar and looked around. "I don't see anything here."

"It's behind the bar. On the wall. Where the mirror used to be."

Quickly reaching the point of exasperation, Clint went behind the bar and started looking. There was no mirror, but there was a dusty frame with some jagged pieces of cracked glass still sticking out in some places. Besides that, there was only the wall and a whole lot of dust.

Keeping his eyes on the gunman and his senses open for a trap, Clint said, "There's nothing here."

"Lower right corner. Look for three scratches pointing toward the corner."

Clint wondered if he wasn't making one hell of a mistake by following this guy's orders. Then again, he felt the pang of curiosity that had led him into the saloon when he spotted the three scratches right where the gunman said they would be.

The marks looked like an animal had clawed at the wall behind where the mirror had been. When Clint touched them, he felt a part of the wall move beneath his finger. Every one of his instincts went on the alert as he prepared himself for some kind of booby trap, but he couldn't feel or hear anything moving around him.

He did, however, feel the scratched wall move inward with just a little bit of pressure. The panel moved inward less than a quarter of an inch and once it stopped, there was a muted click ... a larger part of the wall came loose.

"Pull it," the gunman said from behind him.

Clint used the scratched section as a handhold and pulled the wall outward. The larger section swung out like the door of a cabinet, revealing several bottles of liquor and a few ceramic jugs. Looking over his shoulder, he could see the gunman looking at him with wide, anxious eyes.

"That's the one," the wounded man said excitedly. "Get me a bottle of the good stuff there on the end. I'd sell out my own kin for a couple swigs of that."

Taking one of the bottles, Clint removed the cork and passed it under his nose. He wasn't an expert on whiskey, but he knew the good stuff when he smelled it. And after a whiff of that cork, he was tempted to take a drink for himself. Instead, he passed the bottle over to the man laying on the floor.

Snatching the bottle for his own as though his very life depended on it, the gunman took a long, greedy pull of the liquor. Before he could take another drink, his hand was stopped as Clint took hold of his wrist.

"You've had your drink," Clint said as he wrenched the bottle away. "Now say what you wanted to say."

"You'll give me the rest of that?"

"If it's good enough."

Without hesitation, the gunman nodded.

THIRTEEN

"First of all," the gunman said, "you saw that compartment where the liquor was kept?"

"Yeah."

"This town's full of things like that."

"Liquor cabinets?"

"No! Doors like that! Tunnels and such. Mr. Mason was puttin' them in for years. I hear that his daddy started it before that . . . to make it so he could get away from the law or that others could pay to get away when the law was after them."

Clint nodded. "Like a type of Underground Railroad?"

"I don't know if it was used durin' the war, but it's something like that."

"And who is this Mr. Mason?"

"Alonzo Mason. He's the mayor of this town. He's the one who keeps it so's we can live here on our own without anyone taking notice that we're even here."

"Who's *we*?"

"All of us that still live here."

"You're all outlaws?"

"Not all of us. We just like our town, that's all. And we like it quiet. Mr. Mason keeps it nice and quiet and

53

we don't have to pay taxes or nothin'. We don't need any law and we don't need anyone comin' round poking their noses into our affairs." The gunman said that last part with an obvious distaste for the face he was talking to. That sneering look faded away real quickly once Clint stared him down for a second or two.

"Where are all these others? I didn't even see anyone walking the streets. Do you hole up somewhere in another part of town?"

"We saw you comin' and hid ourselves." The gunman tilted his head and shot Clint an overly confident smile. "You wouldn't be able to find none of us without knowin' where to look. Even the ones who don't . . ." Suddenly, he cut his words off and looked away.

"Go on."

The gunman gritted his teeth and stared toward the bottle still clenched in Clint's hand. Clint let the whiskey go so the man on the floor could take a couple more greedy swallows.

Breathing as though he'd just learned how, the gunman swiped the back of his hand across his mouth and let the firewater work its way through his system.

Clint reached down and snatched the bottle away before too much more of it was lost down the wounded man's gullet. All he needed to do from there was shoot the guy a stern look for the gunman to know what he needed to do next.

"There's other folks livin' here," the gunman said reluctantly. "It started out as family and such that wanted to move on when Mr. Mason wanted to stay."

"His family?"

Nodding, the gunman said, "Yeah. It started that way . . . but there was others. Some of them said they couldn't just walk away knowing that Mr. Mason would be in charge. They said they'd find the law or even the Army to come in and take him away if he didn't let the rest go in peace. Once Mr. Mason said what he thought of that, they said they'd even come after him themselves."

Although the picture was twisted, Clint was starting to see more of it as the gunman kept on talking. "And I don't suppose Mr. Mason thought too much about threats like those."

"Hell no," the gunman replied with no small amount of pride. "He told them that they'd only be making the biggest mistake of their lives doin' something like that. Even gave them another chance to leave town without another cross word bein' said."

"But they didn't take it?"

"Nah. They came at us after the last batch of wagons left town. Me and some of the others who have worked with Mr. Mason didn't want to see some bunch of troublemakers come in and ruin what we was gonna build, so we stood by him and fought them off. We coulda even killed them all, but Mr. Mason held us back. That's the kind of man he is."

Clint didn't respond to the defensive look on the other man's face. It was hard enough for him to keep from saying what he truly thought about what kind of man Mr. Mason sounded like to him. Clint's silence was taken the way he'd intended and the gunman went on, assuming he'd made his point clearly enough.

"But if we couldn't kill them," the gunman continued, "we couldn't just let them all ride away. Not after them makin' threats to go fetch the law and all."

After talking to the wounded man for so long, Clint's instincts were screaming at him to get moving and get away from the saloon where anyone with ears knew there had been shots fired. Also, knowing that the other men could come and go without making a sound through secret tunnels and passages tended to make Clint a little jumpier than normal. "So where are they?"

The gunman took a breath and looked up at Clint with

a certain look in his eye. Either the whiskey was having an effect on him or he was just under the false impression that he held the leverage in the conversation. "They're around. Here and there. Like I said before . . . you'll never find 'em. Why? Did you know someone who lived here?"

Clint had met a few of the people in town the last time he'd been through, but he couldn't remember any names right offhand. What did get to him when he heard that last question, however, was some of the faces he remembered of those locals. Just the fact that he could picture them and that town when it was alive and thriving made the entire situation seem that much more pressing.

If the gunman was telling the truth, then there was something very, *very* wrong taking place. More than that, there were innocent people who were forced to pay for some twisted man's whims. By the way he'd been greeted himself, Clint was certain that Mr. Mason had sprung such traps before . . . and that plenty of others hadn't made it out alive.

"Show me one of these passages you were talking about," Clint said.

FOURTEEN

Clint knew he didn't have much time.

Every moment that slipped by was noticed and missed. After spending the last few days in that town, Clint had gotten used to the practice of absorbing everything he could with every sense he had. He also knew to take nothing for granted. After all, a simple assumption was what had landed him in the situation to begin with.

He'd thought the town was deserted. He'd thought the water in the troughs was clean. He'd thought it would kill some time to take a look inside what appeared to be nothing more than a deserted saloon.

Now, hanging from the underside of a cellar door, Clint could only shake his head at how wrong those assumptions had turned out to be. Actually, he couldn't even shake his head. The rope had chewed away enough of his skin in that area that it even hurt to swallow anymore. At least he was still alive. There was always comfort to be taken from that.

The man who looked more like a rat was still there as well. As far as Clint could tell, that one was going to stay there and watch him die just as he'd promised. The simple truth was that Clint hoped the skinny man would do just that, since that would let him keep his eye on at least one of Mason's men.

As he stood in place and watched Rat-man play with his shovel, Clint kept working at his restraints and doing everything possible to keep his strength up. Staying on his feet was getting to be a task in itself. After all the time he'd spent on them, his legs were turning rubbery and unsteady. The soles of his feet were aching and even shifting them beneath his weight was enough to send jolts of pain up through his entire body.

Consciousness was beginning to fade. As much as he hated to admit it, Clint was having a hard time keeping his eyes open, no matter how much he knew he had to keep doing just that. It didn't show in his eyes or features, but Clint knew that Rat-man was right. If things kept going the way they were, it wouldn't be long before that shovel would get put to use.

There was a long way to go before hunger or thirst would take him, but the rope around his neck and the weight of his own body would do the job just as well and in a fraction of the time. But that thought was just a burr under Clint's saddle. It dug at his skin and kept him awake, but wasn't about to be the death of him.

Not then.

Not ever.

It wasn't about to come to that. Although Clint had never been in such a dangerous and odd situation, he was going to be damned if he was about to give up. All the same . . . the seconds were still ticking by and every last one of them was precious.

As if picking up on all the things that were going through Clint's head, the ratlike man moved forward, dragging the shovel as though it had been nailed to his hand. He got up close enough for Clint to smell the rank mixture of alcohol and rotten milk on his breath and smiled his ugly smile.

"What do you say?" Rat-man asked. "You want me to save us both a little time and kill you right now?"

Clint didn't say a word. Instead, he pulled up all the anguish and pain he was feeling and focused it into a gaze that made the skinny man back up a step. Even restrained, Clint made the rat-man think twice before getting into his face like that.

Saving some of his dignity, Rat-man bared his teeth. He did not, however, try to get so close to Clint again. "I think I should kill you. I'm sick of lookin' at yer face."

"Those weren't your orders," Clint said in a voice so raspy it even took him a little by surprise.

"I know what my orders were! You ain't got to tell me about nothin' like that!"

"Then decide what you're going to do. Either swing that shovel or back the hell off of me. I'm sick of looking at *your* face."

Clint was a firm believer that his poker playing affected so much more of his life than just the nights spent sitting around a table with cards in his hands. Times like this only strengthened that belief. It was because of his ability to read people's faces that Clint could all but hear the thoughts that were going through Rat-man's head.

He could tell the skinny man with the shovel wanted to hit him so badly he could taste it. Clint also knew that eventually, the order would come down to kill him if he didn't die on his own.

But as far as killing him at that very moment, Clint could also tell that Rat-man was bluffing. He wanted to rake in those chips, but he simply didn't have the cards. Judging by the look on the skinny man's face, Clint was dead-on.

"Nah," Rat-man said. "I think I'll wait here and watch you die slow."

Having called that bluff and dodging an appointment with death in the space of a couple seconds, Clint gave

himself a moment to relax. He couldn't exactly close his
eyes and take a much-needed nap, but he could ease off
a bit when it came to Rat-man. They both knew their
places for the time being and there was no need to test
the limits.

Unlike the restraints holding Clint to the wall the ties
keeping back the two men weren't about to weaken in the
near future.

When he thought about the restraints, Clint had to pull
in a deep breath and force his body to obey the command
it so desperately wanted to ignore. He had to keep tensing
his muscles and pulling at the rings. He had to keep
clenching his jaw and straining his neck against the rope.
There were no two ways about it. As much as it hurt and
as tired as he was, he simply had to keep doing those
things.

It felt like he'd been doing nothing but those things for
weeks, even months. Although there had been some progress, Clint suddenly got an idea of what the rat-man was
doing down in that cellar with him.

When he tensed the muscles in his arm and pushed
against the ring, he felt the metal give ever so slightly.
When it did, there was a slight, grating squeal as iron
scraped against iron. The noise wasn't much, but it was
enough to snap Rat-man's head to attention.

Without lifting his head, Clint let out a breath that was
filled with all the fatigue he'd been holding back for so
many hours. He kept it small and mainly in the back of
his throat, but he also managed to mimic the sound of the
metal convincingly enough to put Rat-man's mind somewhat at ease.

The next half hour or so was spent with Clint keeping
quiet and trying to "hold back" his increasingly difficult
breaths. He could tell that Rat-man thoroughly enjoyed
the show and even started relaxing himself once he was

sure that the light inside Clint Adams was finally beginning to flicker and fade away.

Clint forced back the grin that threatened to creep onto his face. Once again skills he'd learned while playing poker had come through to save his life. This time, it was the fine art of bluffing that allowed him to work against his restraints right under the nose of the man who had been sent to guard him.

Keeping his own game face on, Clint continued with what he was doing. All the while, he managed to make Rat-man think that he had the next hand so far in the bag that he was already starting to figure out ways to spend the winnings.

That was exactly where Clint wanted that one: confident and relaxed. After all, if he played his own cards right, Clint figured he could turn this around to one of the most satisfying wins he'd felt in a long time.

FIFTEEN

When Clint had finished his talk with the wounded gunman in the saloon, he figured he'd gotten a pretty solid handle on the way things were in the newly renamed town of Mason. Of course, that opinion would have changed drastically if he would've known exactly where he'd wind up a few days later.

But in the saloon, at that particular time, Clint had yet to see any root cellars or finely crafted devices made for stringing a man up and killing him as slowly as possible. All he knew was what he'd seen and what he'd gathered from the gunman who was still lying on the floor. Clint was more than happy to give the wounded man his bottle and let him think that he'd managed to come out of the gunfight smelling like a rose.

That thought had about two seconds to settle into the gunman's brain. As soon as Clint handed over the bottle and walked away, the gunman lifted the whiskey to his mouth and tipped the bottle back for a large swallow. He was enjoying the victory drink so much that he never even felt Clint's fist as it came down from above him and cracked him right in the face.

With that one shot, Clint was able to knock out the

gunman's lights. Clint was even fast enough to catch the bottle before it dropped out of the other man's hand and broke against the ground. After all, it wouldn't do to make so much noise when he knew that he almost certainly had an audience.

Clint might not have been a doctor, but he knew the gunman's injuries weren't life-threatening. Ironically enough, it was the fact that the man himself had kept alert and awake for so long that had convinced Clint of that very thing. Now that the gunman was taking a little nap, Clint placed the bottle back into the hidden cabinet and walked over to the spot that he'd been shown as the location of one of those secret passages.

Although knocking out the other man before confirming the location of the secret door first was a bit of a gamble, Clint had read the other man's face well enough to take the chance. He walked over to a section of wall next to the front end of the bar and started looking for the knothole that the gunman had pointed out less than a couple minutes ago.

The knothole was precisely where it was supposed to be and when Clint placed his fingers against it and pushed in and down, he felt a small section give way. Even as he looked at the wall with his own two eyes, Clint almost wasn't able to see part of the wall give way. The panel fit so perfectly in place and moved so subtly that it was hardly noticeable.

The section did push inward though, but only just enough for Clint's fingers to reach into the wall and lift up. From there, the larger panel was unlocked and able to be pushed inward with hardly any effort whatsoever. The recessed hinges were so smooth that the panel barely even made a sound as it moved aside, allowing Clint to step into the darkened passage beyond.

Clint shook his head in admiration of the device itself. He'd seen a couple of hidden compartments, but nothing

as intricate as this. In fact, that door was so secret he
doubted if he would have been able to find it even if he'd
had only a vague notion of where to look. All he could
think as he left the saloon behind was how glad he was
that he hadn't lost that gamble he'd taken with the gunman. It would have only been too easy to be steered the
wrong way.

If the rest of the town was filled with doors and compartments like that one, it was no wonder they'd gone
undiscovered for so long. But Clint had found the door
and the gamble had paid off. That meant he might be able
to find the other ones a little easier.

Actually it wasn't even the doors that bothered Clint.
He was more concerned with finding the people who were
being held prisoner by this Mr. Mason. Clint knew that
there was just as good a chance that those people were
already dead, if they even existed at all. But even if there
was a tiny chance that the gunman was telling the truth,
Clint couldn't risk just leaving those people to a fate like
that. It wasn't just what the gunman said that had convinced him, however. It was the way he'd said it that
caused Clint to feel in his gut that there was some truth
in his words.

For that reason alone, he decided against putting the
entire town along with its mess behind him. But there was
something else as well. There was something else that
caused him to move onward into the darkness, through a
passage that had been so expertly hidden away from the
rest of the world.

It was the same thing that had dragged his carcass into
the saloon at first. Quite simply, Clint was curious. Even
after all the shooting and the minor wounds he had acquired in the meantime, Clint was still curious.

He wondered if he wasn't just pushing his luck as he
kept going through the darkness. Perhaps he was still
headed straight into another trap and would never see the

light of day again. For all he knew, the passage emptied out into a pit full of sharpened stakes that hunters used to catch tigers and lions and such.

Before he went too much farther, Clint reached into his shirt pocket and removed a match, which he then struck against the wall. The passage lit up for a brief second as the match started to spark. One more strike was all he needed to get the little flame going as well as a better idea of where he was headed.

Luck was still with him, since the first thing he saw was that he'd been less than a couple steps away from heading straight into another wall. The passage was so quiet that his own footsteps seemed to be swallowed up by the stillness. A couple insects scurried away from the meager light and Clint stepped around the corner he'd been approaching.

The light from the match was too weak for him to see farther than three or four feet in front of him, so the end of the passage could have been anyone's guess.

"This is crazy," he whispered to himself.

Just as Clint was about to turn around and head back, he heard something that made him freeze in place. His ears perked up and he stared ahead even though he could see nothing but inky blackness.

It was a voice.

It was weak and barely audible, but it was most definitely a voice.

Shaking his head as well as his hand as the match burned down to his fingers, Clint kept his steps light and moved ahead.

SIXTEEN

Damn near every room that had been built in the town of Mason had more than one entrance. There were the entrances that could be seen and then there was at least one that couldn't. It hadn't started out that way, of course. No town is built from the ground up with things like secret passages and doors riddling the buildings like so many termite trails. It took a while for something like that to take shape.

But take shape it had. And the reason for that shaping was because of one thing: Alonzo Mason wanted it that way.

Sitting in a padded chair with a back that rose up a foot and a half beyond his own head, Mr. Mason reclined and rolled a thin cigar between his thumb and forefinger, savoring the taste as it soaked into his lips. The town had finally taken shape. It had finally been made to fit his very demanding specifications. And after years of hard work from his own bare hands, he'd finally claimed it for his own.

There had been some luck involved, to be sure. As he'd toiled from building to building under the guise of making extensive repairs and renovations he'd wondered to himself how the town could be even more perfect once he had exclusive access to every last corner of it.

How, he wondered, could he make things even better once he was done expanding on the tunnels and secrets that were already shot through a good portion of the town?

The answer was always there, right on the tip of his tongue, but he'd been too afraid to truly acknowledge it. It was a simple answer, yet something that he thought he shouldn't dare contemplate.

The only way the town could be entirely perfect was if he could rid it of all the undesirables that infested it like so many rats in an otherwise fine ship. If he could somehow clean out the buildings and streets of all the prying eyes that watched him when he wanted to go about his business, he could truly say the town was just right.

That feeling had grown and grown, until finally budding into full bloom when the first unhappy words had begun to drift through the local population. The wells were drying up. Bad news indeed. There was gold and silver to be found in neighboring states. How wonderful. The cattle companies had struck a deal with other drivers who refused to change their routes. How terrible.

Mason smiled. How terrible indeed.

All it had taken was a few well-timed fires, a new band of outlaws raiding the nearby roads, and a few other convenient instances before living in West Bend was simply more trouble than it was worth. And once that became the mood of the masses, all Mason had to do was sit back and wait.

And he didn't even have to wait very long. Within the space of a month or two, all the sheep had packed up their things and were on their way to greener pastures. Mason was left with a small group of his own who shared his vision and were there to take care of the relatively minor problems that remained.

He was able to finish his modifications in peace and soon the town was exactly what he'd always wanted: a shell. It was a piece of scenery in a play that he wrote and directed. It was a run-down shambles that caused people to move along and leave him alone. And if they didn't move on fast enough . . . he had his little group of troublemakers to either convince them to move along or bury them in a field out of sight.

Mason sat in his room, one of the few with no visible entrances whatsoever, and grinned at how well his life was going. And just when he thought it couldn't be any better, one of the walls moved inward and a thin brunette stepped into his sanctum.

As soon as she was out of the darkness, she lifted her chin and turned her large, dark eyes toward Mason. "I was hoping you'd be here," she said.

"Is that so? And why's that?"

"There's someone in town. An intruder."

"I know," Mason replied without more than passing interest reflected in his tone. "Morgan told me about it a while ago. Didn't the others take care of him yet?"

The brunette stepped closer and set the lantern she'd been carrying on the edge of Mason's desk. Its light died away as she twisted the knob before walking around the desk and standing directly beside Mason himself. "They got the drop on him. They even got a few shots off, but they didn't kill him."

Mason looked more than confused. He looked as though he didn't understand the words that were coming out of her mouth. "Why not? Why wouldn't they kill him? That's what I told them to do."

"They tried, but . . ."

"How many intruders are there?"

"Just one."

"And I sent four men after him, didn't I?"

She nodded, keeping her eyes on him as he raised up

out of his chair and stabbed out the cigar into an ashtray. Her arms reached out for him, gliding along the sides of his shoulders and moving down to his hands, which hung precariously close to a gun strapped around his waist. When she reached the weapon, she drew in a quick breath as though the pistol had somehow reached out to touch her instead.

"What do you want me to do?" she asked.

"Send someone out after him. Better yet, send Luke."

Nodding, the brunette went over to another of the blank spots on the walls and tapped twice. A second later, the door swung open to reveal a parlor that was filled with lush carpeting and fine furniture. A man waited outside and listened to the hastily whispered orders given to him by the attractive woman.

Once she was done, the brunette turned and shut the door behind her. "What do you want me to do now?" she asked, while walking slowly back to where Mason was standing.

"I want that intruder killed."

"Should I do it myself? Should I find him and shoot him without waiting for anyone else?" Lifting her leg, she placed the ball of her foot on the edge of his desk. From there, she placed the tips of her fingers on her ankles and eased them up along her calf while pulling up the hem of her skirt.

Mason watched her with increasing interest. His eyes jumped from her full lips, down to her pert breasts, and down to the leg that was revealed as her dress was slowly peeled up and out of the way. His breaths came quicker when she reached her knee and started rubbing her thigh with slow, massaging strokes of her hands.

"Should I shoot him myself?" she asked as the edge of her thumb grazed along the bottom of the little holster strapped around her thigh. "You want me to shoot him with this gun?"

Mason reached out and placed his hand upon her knee, moving his palm over the collected folds of her skirt that were gathered there. When he slid his hand down to her bare skin, he could see the way her eyes narrowed slightly in anticipation of his next move.

That brought a smile to his face, which only grew as he let his hand wander down over the smooth skin of her thigh to where the derringer was kept. "I want you to keep that gun right where it is. But these," he said, sliding his fingers to the undergarments she wore, "these have got to go."

She positioned herself so she could sit on the edge of the desk, spreading her legs to allow Mason to get in between them. "I can't do everything on my own, can I?"

That was all she needed to say before Mason all but tore the panties from her body.

SEVENTEEN

"You like that, don't ya, Paula?"

Mason spoke the question without really asking it. He could read the answer in the way she looked back at him and breathed a little quicker as the undergarments were pulled away from beneath her skirt. But he asked her all the same, mainly because he wanted to hear her respond in that low, sexy voice of hers.

"I like it," Paula groaned. "You know I like it."

Letting the brunette's panties drop to the floor, Mason kept his hand between her legs, rubbing along the skin that had already grown hot and moist to his touch. He explored her body with his hand, tracing a line along the inside of her thighs, all the way up to the slick folds of delicate skin between them.

Arching her back as she felt his fingers roam through the thatch of hair between her legs, Paula hooked her leg around Mason's waist and moved her hips in a slow, grinding circle against his fingers. Leaning her head back, she allowed her thick brown hair to fall behind her as waves of sensation moved through her body. When Mason's touch found the sensitive nub of her clitoris, she snapped her eyes open and let out a sharp, delighted moan.

He loved watching her squirm and writhe in front of him. Almost as much as he loved touching the sensuous brunette, Mason loved watching her as she was overtaken by pleasure. He'd watched her several times while wandering his hidden halls and peeking in through the holes he'd drilled.

Several times, Mason had watched as Paula touched herself when she thought she was alone or took slow, luxurious baths in her private room. He thought of those moments even when he had her pressed up against him, begging him with her eyes to indulge every one of his desires.

Only part of Mason was moving his hands beneath her skirt and pulling open the buttons that closed over her breasts. The other part of him was picturing the moment as if he was watching it from behind a wall, leering in the darkness.

Paula put a foot on Mason's chair and pushed herself up farther onto the desk. Once there, she started unbuttoning his shirt and tearing open the front of his pants. Her hands moved roughly over him, stripping his belt away before tugging down his pants and reaching inside to grasp his hardening penis.

Mason didn't get the dress all the way off of her. Instead, he pulled down the top of her blouse and clasped his hands on her breasts so he could squeeze the erect nipples between his fingers. Her breasts were small and soft in his grasp and she moaned loudly as he roughly moved his hands over them.

Her hands moved quickly as well, stroking his shaft vigorously to keep pace with the insistent way she felt his hands on her. The harder and faster she worked him, the more erect he got until finally she knew he was ready to be inside of her.

Mason stepped back and guided the tip of his cock between her legs. Before entering her, he took hold of her hips and pulled her forward so that she had to hold on to him to keep from falling. He liked the momentary look of fear on her face as she thought he might let her drop. It made his penis even more rigid when he knew that she was relying on him to keep her from getting hurt while she was at her most vulnerable.

Paula's heart fluttered inside her chest as she felt Mason's strong hands close around her hips. He moved her roughly over the desk and seemed as though he was about to toss her across the room. He was a strong man and Paula knew that he was capable of using that strength in many terrible ways. The strange, faraway look in his eyes did nothing to assuage the fears that always crept into her mind at these times.

But he didn't throw her down. Mason kept her perched on the desk and moved in closer. "I want you to put it in," he commanded.

Reaching down, she took hold of his cock and stroked it all the way up and down its length. She smiled warmly, knowing that she was touching him the way he liked, but stopped when she saw the flash of anger in his eyes.

"That's not what I told you to do," he snarled.

The tone of his voice was a familiar one, but it was also tinted with a real edge that went beyond the rough playing they engaged in at moments like these. Paula moved her fingers all the way down to the base of his shaft and guided him toward the moist lips of her vagina.

Once he felt himself slide into her warm wetness, Mason let out a satisfied grunt and pushed himself all the way inside of her. He grabbed her hips and pulled her forward while thrusting with nearly all of his strength.

Paula let out a grunt as well. At first she was surprised with how roughly he was moving, but once he began pumping in and out, she clamped her arms around his neck and moved her body to the rhythm he'd set. The feel of his insistent thrusts made the moment all the more intense and the digging of his fingers into her hips added a certain spice to the sensations that washed over her.

It wasn't long before Mason felt her taking some of the control away from him. He resisted at first when he felt himself being pulled forward. But he gave in once he saw the way she leaned back and stretched out on top of the desk. Her little breasts were displayed proudly and the way she opened her legs for him made him want to do nothing but give in.

Paula reached out with both hands and swept away all the loose items she could get to. Pens, papers and the ashtray dropped to the floor in a loud clatter as she inched back so she could pull him on top of her. From there, it didn't take much to get Mason to climb up onto the desk.

Although he didn't appreciate being led by her, Mason let his instincts take over as he looked down at her naked body spread out before him. He reached down to cup her breasts and then grab hold of her legs. She let herself be handled by him, moaning when he leaned down and started kissing her roughly on the neck and chest.

Propping one foot on the edge of the desk, Paula set her other ankle upon Mason's shoulder; running her fingernails down the front of his chest. She recognized the almost feral look in his eyes as he situated himself between her legs and drove inside of her. As his cock was buried all the way to its base, they both groaned loudly as their excitement hit its peak.

Mason grabbed her shoulder with one hand and reached around to cup her backside with the other. Once he had her firmly in his grasp, he began pounding into her with so much force that the desk began to move slightly beneath them.

Paula was wet enough to keep him gliding easily in and out, allowing her to lean back and enjoy feeling every inch of him drive into her body. She pumped her hips in time, trying to keep up with his quick, intense rhythm. When she leaned her head back, it was hanging in midair since her shoulders were resting on the edge of the desk. Closing her eyes and groaning as the sensations pulsed through her flesh, she let him ride her as roughly as he wanted, taking some forbidden pleasure from the knowledge that she wouldn't have been able to stop him even if she'd wanted to.

Mason liked to think that he was dominating the brunette, even though she was the one who usually instigated their encounters. In his mind, however, he was asserting himself upon her, taking her no matter what she wanted or desired.

And, as always, there was that part of his brain that was watching the pair fucking on top of his desk. That was the part that got him more excited. And when he cried out in the grip of his climax, it was that part of Alonzo Mason that was feeling all the pleasure.

EIGHTEEN

They had been sitting there for weeks.

Or perhaps it had been for months.

Although they doubted it had been as long as years, the seven people had lost all track of time. After all, there was no real way for them to gauge when day passed into night because there wasn't even a way for them to see the sun. There were no clocks and none of the men who came to bring them food were too inclined to talk.

The room they were in was the shape of a perfect rectangle. The cells were lined up three on each side and there weren't even any doors to keep them in. There was no need for doors on the cells since they didn't even know how to open the door of the room itself. All they saw of that was a section of wall that opened up to allow any number of armed men to stream inside.

After watching the armed men come and go enough times, all the seven people knew where the door was, but that was about it. After several failed attempts, the prisoners had given up trying to rush the guards when they came through. Apart from the fact that the men were armed with shotguns, the prisoners had lost their will to fight once their new diet took its effect on them.

Alonzo Mason only allowed them to eat rolls and water. There was never enough to fill them, yet just enough to keep them from starving outright. Their bodies had begun to waste away until getting up from the floor had become a major undertaking.

Now, when the guards paid them a visit, the prisoners simply looked up at them. Sometimes they barely had enough energy to do that much. Besides the six open cells, the rectangular room had a couple stools bolted to the floor and a rickety cot with some old horse blankets thrown on top of it.

The prisoners had given up trying to ask why Alonzo Mason would keep them there. They'd given up asking how long they'd been held captive and if they were ever going to leave. No answers were ever forthcoming. The only thing that they'd been told was that it was, indeed, Alonzo Mason who was in charge.

In fact, mentioning that name was the only thing that had ever gotten a prisoner out of the rectangular room. Of course, that still didn't mean it was something anyone was anxious to do again.

Andy was a tall, big-boned man in his late twenties. Of all the prisoners now held in that room, he was the one who'd given the guards the hardest time. In fact, he'd even managed to kill one of the gunmen who'd jumped him in the streets of West Bend and it wasn't until after a prolonged fight that he'd been dragged down and tossed into that room.

For that reason alone, the other prisoners had insisted on letting him sleep on the cot for the duration of his stay. Two little children, one boy and one girl, had looked up to him as they would a father. Part of the reason for that was because of the admirable way he'd struggled against the mean guards who treated them like animals. Another part of that was because their real father had been killed

right in front of them when they'd been captured on the
streets of the town outside.

The two women who were being held captive shrugged
away from Andy out of pure reflex. Because he was a
male they'd never seen before they instinctually feared
him as they would the guards, who had always tormented
them by describing the dirty, degrading things they
wanted to do if the mood ever struck them.

There were two men in the room as well and they
looked at Andy with respect when they saw the blood on
his hands as well as the looks of hatred thrown at him
from the armed guards. Those two prisoners could tell
what Andy must have done. And for that, they immediately did their best to ease his suffering.

Leaning back against the wall, Andy rubbed his right
shoulder and winced as the all-too-familiar pain lanced
through his body. As much as he tried to forget about
what had happened when he'd been brought into that
room, those memories were also the only things he had
of the outside world.

The last time he'd seen the sky, Andy had been wincing
in pain just as he was while leaning against the wall in
his regular spot. He'd been wincing then because the gunmen were shooting the other three deputies that he'd
brought with him to face down the killer responsible for
burning down houses and murdering innocent travelers.

Andy had come back to West Bend with the law on his
side, thinking that that would be enough to win the day
and take back what had been stolen. But the killers had
been hidden too well and they had surprise on their side
to such a degree that none of the lawmen even suspected
the town held anything but ghosts once they'd arrived.

But there were more than ghosts.

There were rifles and pistols and enough lead to fill the
air like hail as the deputies were picked off like bottles
from a fence. Andy had barely managed to survive a cou-

ple minutes. He'd gotten enough of his wits about him to
return fire, even drill one killer through the head, but that
still wasn't enough.

Once the killers had finished with the deputies, they
turned their sights onto him. They disarmed him and then
proceeded to make him pay for the one killer that Andy
had managed to hit. They made him pay in blood and
pain.

First they beat him to within an inch of his life.

Next, they sliced off three of his fingers.

Finally, they wrenched his arm out of his socket before
dragging him through a wall and into the dark.

After that, Andy's memories started to fade. It had been
a mercy that he'd passed out, but any thankfulness he
might have felt instantly disappeared when he'd awakened
to find where he was.

That seemed so long ago. Judging by the faces of the
prisoners gathered in that rectangular room, every one of
them had already died a couple times. But something still
burned within them that kept them going to see another
day.

It didn't matter that they didn't know when one day
ended and another began. Even the youngest among those
seven were determined to keep going. They, like all the
others, still had something inside of them that would not
allow them to let the sneering faces of the guards get to
them.

Andy had made sure to fan that common flame as best
he could. He felt the hope within himself just as surely
as he recognized it in the others. Even then, as he leaned
back against the wall and rubbed the portion of his shoulder that had healed crooked despite all the help of his
fellow prisoners, Andy could feel hope.

Fighting back the painful expression as best he could,
Andy looked over and saw that both the children were
looking at him. He smiled at the young ones, which

caused them both to immediately look away. Neither of those kids had talked yet, but they didn't have to say a word for Andy to know what they were thinking.

They looked to him as a leader. He didn't know why, but all of the others did. And although it was an honor, Andy couldn't help but feel a little ashamed that he couldn't do any more to live up to their expectations. The two women divvied out some bread that they'd been saving as part of their daily ritual to the two men who were asleep on the floor.

Andy bit back his pain and gave his thanks when one of the women came by to hand him some food.

"You think they might slip up today?" she asked, referring to the mistake they were all waiting for from one of the guards.

Andy forced a smile onto his face and nodded. "Maybe."

NINETEEN

The passage reminded Clint of being in a mine shaft. There was the strange feeling that he was falling, which came from not being completely sure of where he was taking his next step. There was the complete and total darkness that even seemed to close in around the feeble light given off by the matches he would strike. And of course there was the sensation that the walls themselves were closing in around him from all sides.

Clint might have been keeping track of how many steps he took and roughly how far he'd gone, but it still seemed like twice that distance. There were two very distinct things that were very unlike a mine. First of all, the walls were perfectly formed and smooth. Second, it was relatively clean.

There was some dust, which couldn't be avoided, but no more than would be expected in such a closed-in space. Clint had been expecting everything from insects to layers of filth, but the passage seemed no less dirty than an attic. At the very least, thinking about such mundane things served to keep his mind off the sense that he was trapped deep underground in some kind of large coffin.

These thoughts also made the time slip by a little faster,

keeping him just a little distracted until there was something to capture every bit of his attention. He'd heard
them just a little while ago, which made Clint slow his
steps down somewhat.

Voices.

It was impossible to say whether or not they were coming from a couple feet or several yards away. The walls
of the passage were so well sealed that the only thing
Clint could hear clearly was his own boots scraping
against the ground. When he needed to strike a match, the
sound reverberated like a rake being dragged across
wooden boards. And now that he had something outside
to listen for, Clint realized once again just how tightly the
passage had been constructed.

The gunman at the saloon had told Clint he might have
to walk a ways, but Clint figured he wouldn't have to go
any farther than the length of the actual building. He may
have been walking slowly, but Clint knew for certain that
he'd covered more area than what could be contained in
the saloon.

Rather than try to figure any more of it out on his own,
Clint kept his mind focused on what was ahead, knowing
the explanations were up there somewhere.

Striking the last of his supply of matches, Clint walked
about five more feet before he saw that the tunnel ended
directly ahead.

The voices were getting louder now, and he was just
barely able to make out what some of them were saying.
That was only due to the fact that one of the speakers was
screaming loud enough to wake the dead.

"How many more do you need?" came the loud, yet
still somewhat muffled voice.

The ones that followed were more quiet and too faint
to be heard clearly from where Clint was standing. He
could, however, tell that the ones who were keeping their

voices down were doing so because they were too scared to match the first man's tone.

It didn't take an expert judge of character to be able to smell the fear that was soaked into the cowed responses that followed. The mumbled replies painted pictures in Clint's head of children standing with their heads hung low or dogs too afraid to look their master in the eye.

"I got other things to do!" said the first man. His voice was lowered somewhat, but there was still enough steam behind it to push through the tightly sealed passage. "You go and you find him . . ."

Some of that was lost, but Clint got the general idea.

Footsteps thumped over the floor in front of Clint and beyond the end of the passage. As the flame died out in Clint's hand, the only move he made was a quick flick of his wrist to keep his flesh from getting singed. Once again, darkness claimed the space around him and for the first time, Clint allowed himself to become one with the shadows rather than try to see through them.

The heavy footsteps got closer, but then turned back and began to fade. Whoever it was had started to regain his temper since more of his words weren't making it through the wall.

"Kill . . . Mason will take your . . . and . . . into mush."

Again, Clint got the general idea.

TWENTY

Clint found with a little trial and error that he could move all the way up to the end of the passage without making a sound. It wasn't so much that he was light on his feet, but the boards were fit so tightly together that there was no room for any squeaks to be made. Besides making it easier for him to move, it also explained how those other gunmen in the saloon had been able to sneak up on him.

Focusing on the sound of the mumbling voices, Clint stepped up to the end of the passage and put his ear against the wall. It allowed him to catch a few more words, but not enough to piece together much meaning. More important, he could tell that whoever had been yelling threats was now gone.

None of the remaining voices had that commanding presence. All of them, however, were doing their best to talk tough without making too much noise of their own. After adjusting to the sound of the voices through the wall, Clint eventually started to pick up a few things. Finally, like eyes that had adjusted to darkness, his ears could hear a good portion of what was being said. From what he could hear, Clint figured there were at least three other men remaining in the next room.

"So where do you think he went?" one of the men asked.

"Out of the saloon, I know that much. Probably gone. I think he was hurt when them shots was fired."

". . . not gone. Not unless he ran off without his horse. Ain't nobody would leave . . . damn fine animal."

There was some laughter and the shuffling of feet.

"Luke wants that horse for himself . . . have to get it quick or someone might just beat him to it."

". . . steal from Luke?"

"He ain't so bad. Just . . . of hot air, is all. Only a matter of time before . . . comes to his senses and hands . . . over to someone else who don't scream so much."

More laughter, except it was a little more nervous this time around. Even in the darkness, Clint could almost picture those three men looking over their shoulders to make sure nobody else could hear them. He shook his head, but suddenly froze when he picked up the next bit of conversation.

After a couple of footsteps that seemed to close in on where Clint was standing, there was the creak of weight being pressed against the wall. Judging by how much clearer the voice was, Clint could only guess that the speaker was leaning against the same wall he was.

"Which one'a you is gonna check on them prisoners?"

The only problem with having one of the men so close was that the others' voices were muffled that much more. The tones Clint could hear sounded like dissatisfied grunts, which was enough for the moment.

"Well one'a you has to do it, since Mr. Mason wants to keep them alive."

More mumbling, but Clint could pick out one word amid the garbage: *kill.*

"Maybe we should," the closest voice said. "Lord only knows what Mr. Mason wants to keep them around for and it sure would be easier without 'em. Didn't you say

they was looking pretty bad last time?" After waiting for
his response, the voice said, "Me, too. We'll work on it.
If that don't kill 'em then we can take things up on our
own. That way we won't have to wait before making our
move across the state line."

Clint had heard more than enough. Not only did these
men seem to know a hell of a lot more than the one in
the saloon, but they also seemed ready to act against whoever else was trying to boss them around. Three words
went through Clint's mind when he thought of that: divide
and conquer.

Any men ready to go against the man above them in
the chain of command was a weak link. And since he was
fumbling through enemy territory that was secreted within
a deserted town like an anthill hiding beneath a field, Clint
needed to find a way to break the chain as soon as hu-
manly possible.

Clint had learned a lot in his short time within the town
that used to be West Bend. And once he decided to take
on the men at the other side of the wall, he intended to
learn a whole lot more. The first step, however, wasn't
going to be as simple as it might have seemed.

Before he could confront and question those men he'd
been listening to, Clint needed to get on the other side of
the wall. He already knew the boards were fit together
tight enough to keep from squeaking, which made the
corridor he was in that much stronger on every side.

He also knew that whoever had designed the lock-and-
trigger mechanisms had done so with the specific purpose
of keeping them hidden no matter how hard someone
might try to find them. Clint had been hoping that the
designer might make the handles a little more obvious on
the inside of the passage, but after a quick search with his
hands, he realized that had been a little too much to hope
for.

The Colt was still hanging at his side and he knew he

could always blast his way out, but that only guaranteed him a deadly reception once he finally did make it through. After studying the two locks he'd found in the saloon, Clint knew he could find his way out with a little bit of time. The only problem now was that he didn't have *any* time.

If he was going to catch up with those men, he needed to do it pretty damn quickly. The fact that they were already talking about hurting the prisoners only made matters worse.

There was a creak from the wall, telling Clint that whoever was standing against it had moved away. Once he heard that, he felt along the sides and edges of the wooden panel with quick, deftly moving fingers. Considering that the trigger to the entrance had been marked by nothing more than a set of scratches, Clint didn't exactly know what he was looking for.

He tried hunting for any imperfections in the wooden surface, but found too many that could have been possible candidates. He knew that by pressing on too many spots or scraping too hard in one place would only call attention to the fact that he was there.

Suddenly, Clint stopped and took a step back. The answer that presented itself was so simple that he felt a little flustered for not thinking of it before. When he heard the voices start to get muffled, he reached out with his left hand, made a fist . . . and knocked.

TWENTY-ONE

"What was that?"

Just as they'd been about to leave, the men in the back room of what had once been Town Hall froze and turned toward the rear wall. There were five in all and every last one of them stared toward the sharp rapping noise they'd all just heard.

Standing closest to the wall in question, a large man wearing a battered leather vest looked back and forth between the wooden surface and the other men staring at him. "Did the rest of you hear that?"

"Yeah," one of the others said. "It sounded like somethin' scratching back there."

They all waited for a couple seconds for the sound to repeat itself. When it didn't, they all relaxed enough to take their hands away from their pistols. The men farthest away from that wall had already started to leave the room.

"It's probably nothing," one of the men said. "Sometimes a squirrel or something gets caught in one of them tunnels Mr. Mason's so damn proud of. We got things to do, so you can let the damn thing out of there."

The man in the vest scowled for a second and then waved them off with a dismissive hand. "Fine. Get on out of here . . . and don't forget about what we were talking about here. And don't tell anyone else. Not yet, anyway."

Three of the men were already out of the room by that point. "We'll talk later," one of them said over his shoulder. "And keep your own damn mouth shut, as well."

Staring daggers into the backs of the men who left, the man in the vest scowled silently until the others' footsteps could no longer be heard. "I don't know about them, Cam. Mason might have his hooks into 'em just a little too deep for my taste."

The man he was speaking to was of average build and dressed in dirty jeans and a shirt made of material so thin that the weave of the cotton could be seen in various places. "He's got his hooks into all of us," Cam said. "You and me included."

"Shut yer mouth."

"It's the truth and you know it."

Letting the words sink in for a moment, the man in the vest started to nod slowly and walk toward the door. "Maybe you're right. But it's nothin' that's gonna last forever. I don't know about you, but I'm just in this until we head out of this—"

As soon as Clint heard some of the men walk away, he figured he might be able to get out of his current fix a little easier than he'd thought. When the voice of the closest man started to fade, he knew the chances of his plan working were going to fade as well.

He didn't waste another second before reaching out and rapping on the panel in front of him one more time. Clint put a little more force behind it, however, since his first attempt hadn't come through as loudly as he'd wanted.

Clint could hear the men talking, but when he knocked on the panel the second time, both of the voices stopped immediately. So did the retreating footsteps.

●   ●   ●

Both Cam and the man in the vest stopped before leaving the room. The second of those two still had his mouth open in the process of forming the next words in his sentence. Rather than say what he was originally going to, he looked over to Cam and nodded toward the back wall.

He didn't need to say another word before Cam took out his gun and nodded back. Once he drew his own weapon, the man in the vest stepped toward the back wall and listened carefully.

He heard nothing.

He waited . . . and still there wasn't a sound coming from the wall.

Finally, losing his patience for the matter, he reached up with his free hand and pressed in a lightly colored knothole in the wood next to a picture hanging by itself. The knothole slid in only slightly and was followed by a sharp *click*.

The panel started to move inward and was blocked before it could reveal the passageway on the other side.

Shaking his head, the man who'd opened the door pushed on the panel with his shoulder. "Goddamn thing," he muttered while shoving the door back. He put all his weight behind the next push, which was enough to break the door open all the way.

Of course, once the door came open, there was nothing to keep him from charging headfirst into the dark corridor.

As far as Cam could see, his partner had just broken one of Mason's doors and was about to fall flat on his face in the process. Obviously, that was something he wanted to see for himself.

Clint waited for the man in the vest to take one more try at the door, which he'd been holding shut with his boot. When the guy charged into the panel, Clint let it open on its own and stepped back to let the man come straight at him like a stampede.

Although the light streaming into the passage was a little overwhelming compared to the near-total darkness of before, Clint was able to keep himself from being too blinded by squinting and turning away just a bit. He couldn't miss the man who came running toward him through the door.

And he also couldn't miss the gun clenched in the guy's fist.

TWENTY-TWO

The man in the vest charged toward Clint like a bull with its head lowered for the gore. Although he hadn't seen him right away, the incoming gunman wouldn't be able to miss Clint since there wasn't anything else but him in the sealed corridor.

But even if the other man had seen Clint, that fact alone wasn't enough to slow his pace down before Clint stepped forward and made a move of his own.

Grabbing the other man's shirt between the collar and shoulder, Clint used the guy's momentum against him and pivoted on his heels while pulling back. The combination of the speed in the guy's steps along with Clint's redirection diverted the bull's charge and sent him facefirst into the side of the passage.

The other man's skull made a sickening *crunch* when his face met the solidly constructed wood, and was soon followed by the more muffled sound of Clint's knee being buried in his stomach.

Already turning his attention to what else would be coming through that door, Clint held his Colt at the ready while shoving the man in front of him straight down to the floor. When the man in the vest hit the ground, Clint stomped his boot down between his shoulder blades to keep him pinned in place.

"What the hell?" came a voice from the room at the other end of the passage.

Clint's ears were attuned to the thump of boots against floorboards and he immediately picked up on the fact that the second man was on his way into the corridor. The first man, although dazed, was trying to get onto his feet. Clint took his boot off the man's back, set it down on the floor and then lowered himself down to one knee in a classic firing stance. From there, he was also able to press his shin down across the other man's back, which held him down even more securely than before.

Before any shapes could be seen in the doorway, a shot blasted through the room, its thunder growing into an explosion as the sound was amplified within the corridor. The bullet took a chunk out of the door, which was thick enough to divert the lead off its course and send it into the wall several feet away from Clint's position.

Clint lowered his head slightly, but didn't budge from where he was. With so little space at his disposal, he knew better than to abandon his spot before finding another one that he was certain was better. The second man was still coming, so Clint sat tight and waited for him to arrive.

Squirming with all his strength, the man with the vest struggled to get out from under Clint's leg. With a little added pressure, Clint was able to press him down until the guy could barely move. Before he had to worry about that one, however, Cam was just looking in from the other room.

At first, Clint didn't see anything but another shadow. Then, he saw the muzzle of a gun as the light bounced off the dull metal and Cam looked carefully around the corner.

Clint thought the other man was running to his friend's aid, but apparently Cam had thought twice before making

the same mistake as the man in the vest. Even with the
dim lighting inside the corridor, Cam was able to make
out what was going on. At the minimum, he saw enough
to let him know that his friend wasn't on the winning end
of things.

"Who are—" Cam started to ask, but the rest of his
question was drowned out by the roar of his gun, which
filled the corridor like rolling thunder.

Unlike the previous shot, Clint didn't feel comfortable
just waiting in his current spot as this other one went off.
He reflexively ducked his head and shifted forward so he
could lower the rest of his body while pressing down even
harder upon the man trapped beneath him.

After the bullet whipped over his head, Clint pointed
the modified Colt and took a shot of his own. With Cam
standing in between the light and dark, it was hard for
Clint to see if he'd hit the other man or not. His instincts
told him he had, but he wasn't about to bet his life on it,
no matter how good his track record was.

Clint could feel the man in the vest starting to gain
some leverage beneath him. He knew the fallen man's gun
was close by, but he wasn't able to see it in the near-total
darkness. Until this point, he'd been satisfied with keeping
the guy immobile, but now Clint was starting to wonder
how much longer he could pull off that particular trick.

Spouting off a couple choice obscenities, Cam pulled
his trigger again. His shot came closer and might have
actually hit Clint if he would've stayed in his original
spot. But ducking down those extra inches had saved
Clint's life and he was moving once again to make sure
that same life wasn't snuffed out by some punk's lucky
shot.

TWENTY-THREE

"I got you now, you son of a bitch!" Those words came out sounding wet and mushy, since they were being spat out of the mouth that was currently being jammed against the floor.

Clint didn't even have to look to know that the man in the vest had finally found his gun and was just about to take his shot. Even though Clint's leg was still keeping the other man from looking at his target, it would have taken an act of God for him to miss it.

In fact, Clint could practically feel the gun being lifted up and pointed in his direction. It was going to be a point-blank shot and if the man in the vest got to pull his trigger, it was definitely going to hurt.

A lot.

Clint was already moving when he took his next shot. He wasn't aiming at anything except for the general vicinity of where Cam was standing. The Colt barked once in his hand, doing exactly what Clint had intended by making the man in front of him back off and pause before shooting again.

The moment he saw he'd gotten the opening he'd been hoping for, Clint followed through. Beneath him, the man in the vest had already snapped back the hammer of his pistol and was grunting in some premature celebration that sounded less human and more the kind of sound that would come out of a steer as it was being branded.

In the back of his mind, Clint pictured the gun coming up from beneath and behind him. He knew well enough that there was no way he could shoot both that one and Cam before both men were able to fire. He might have been fast, but even Clint Adams had his limits.

Fortunately, Clint didn't intend on shooting both of them in the space of less than a fraction of a second. With Cam still reeling back slightly after nearly getting hit with that last wild shot, Clint kept his body moving forward while tucking his chin in close against his chest.

As he leaned forward, Clint felt his entire body starting to fall toward the floor. He used that motion and forward momentum as a way to get out of Cam's line of fire while delivering one more crushing blow to the other one's back as he rolled completely over the man in the vest like a millstone.

Not only could Clint hear the man below him grunting in pain, he could feel the guy's body compressing beneath his weight as he drove every bit of air from his lungs. The way he maneuvered himself, Clint wouldn't have been surprised if he cracked a few of the other man's ribs as well.

When Clint rolled off of the other man and hit the floor, he kept his momentum going until he was back with his feet beneath him. Aiming from the hip, he pulled the Colt's trigger and sent a round into Cam's upper chest close to his shoulder. He hadn't been trying to kill the guy, but Clint wasn't about to hesitate if his first shot didn't have the desired effect.

"Ow, shit!" Cam grunted as he recoiled in pain. The gun slipped from his hand as pain coursed through his wounded shoulder and flooded that arm. Numbness came soon after that and even if Cam had the presence of mind to take another shot, he wouldn't have been able to keep hold of his gun.

Fortunately for Cam, that had been Clint's desired effect.

Clint spun in a tight half-circle so he could see what the man in the vest was doing. He didn't know if it had been reflex or luck that made him aim the Colt where he did, but when he saw the guy on the floor, he saw that the other man had already gotten his gun back and was ready to fire.

The man in the vest looked like he was hurting, but it wasn't enough for him to give up trying to drop Clint like a bad habit. He gritted his teeth when he tried to turn to get a better look at Clint, but managed to take aim and tighten his finger around his trigger.

Without sparing another thought, Clint aimed as if he was simply pointing his finger at the man in the vest and fired.

The Colt barked once again, filling the corridor with thunder. Once that noise faded, the dark, confined space became deathly quiet. The air was filled with acrid smoke and bits of dust that had been knocked loose during the fight.

The man in the vest was propping himself up at an awkward angle, trying to regain his balance. All he was able to do was keep himself from keeling over and that was with a whole lot of effort. He looked like a statue frozen like that, until finally he let out a shaky breath and let himself fall backward.

The back of his head hit the floor with a solid *thump* and he stayed perfectly still after that. It was the difference between dropping a live animal or a sack of rocks. They both weighed the same, but the life in the first thing caused it to seem lighter and even bounce more when hitting the ground. The sack of rocks hit and stayed right where it fell because it, like the man in the vest, was dead.

Standing up to his full height, Clint stepped back and picked up the gun from the dead man's hand. He released the hammer and tucked the weapon beneath his gun belt. "Kick that gun over here," he said to Cam after turning the Colt in his direction.

Cam glared at Clint with intensity that no amount of shadows could hide. Finally, good sense won out over everything else that was going through him and he sent his gun across the floor with one well-placed boot.

Clint slipped one of his toes beneath the weapon, snapped his leg up and popped the gun up into the air just high enough for him to catch it. He tucked that weapon next to the other one and then nodded toward the door at the end of the passage. "Get moving."

Although Cam shook his head with disgust, he did as he was told.

When Clint stepped out of the passage, he felt as though he'd been cooped up in there for days. Merely getting out again seemed like a victory. Before he took too much time to celebrate, he walked across the room and shut the door that led out into a hallway.

"Are there others nearby?" Clint asked.

Cam shrugged. His tough act lasted another second or two until Clint slowly holstered his weapon and stared him dead in the eyes.

"Two of you couldn't take me out just now," Clint said in a voice that sounded as though it had been forged from pure steel. "And four of you couldn't take me out in that old saloon back there What the hell makes you think you can do better on your own?"

After a moment or two, which was taken purely to salvage some of his pride, Cam said, "There were some others around, but they left."

"How many are in town altogether?"

Although Cam didn't answer right away, Clint could

tell that it wasn't out of purposely wanting to waste time. In fact, Cam's face showed a small degree of nervousness that reminded Clint of a child struggling to guess the right answer after being called upon in school.

"I don't know how many," Cam finally admitted. "Maybe twenty."

Clint didn't have to hear footsteps or see men running down the hall to know his time was limited. So rather than push for details from someone who probably couldn't even count, he started covering everything he needed.

"Show me how that works," Clint said, pointing toward the secret door.

Cam closed the door and showed him the way the knothole slid back and opened the panel.

Nodding, Clint said, "Good. Now let's discuss those prisoners."

TWENTY-FOUR

The air hung inside the rectangular room like a burlap curtain. It laid heavily upon all of the prisoners' shoulders and forced their heads to point down toward the floor. It seemed to suck all the air out of the room and make them feel as though they'd been buried inside a deep hole where they were covered with dirt and forgotten.

Everyone sat in their normal places without saying a word. After all the time they'd spent together, they really didn't have to speak to communicate what they wanted to say. One well-placed look or shrug spoke more than a mouthful of words.

Sometimes, they didn't even have to look at each other for those same points to be made. When they heard the muffled voices outside their wall, they didn't want to speak. Partly because the fear was so thick in the air that there was no possible way to miss it. But also, they didn't want to draw attention to themselves.

The women and children huddled together, keeping every breath quiet and suppressing every whimper. The men had taken up positions as well, tensing their failing muscles in case this was the time when they were either shown a genuine opportunity or forced to play what few cards they had.

Having talked outside for a couple minutes, the voices stopped suddenly and the sound of metal moving within the wall could be heard. It was the familiar sound of the locking mechanism being pulled back and soon the panel in the wall would slide away.

It wasn't time to be fed, which meant there was some other reason for the guards to be there.

Andy looked toward the women and nodded steadily. They returned the gesture and held on to the two children a little tighter. Looking toward the two men, Andy nodded again. This was a different nod, however. It told them to be ready and be strong. Both of them indicated that they understood before shifting to look toward the panel, which moved out from the wall.

By the time the door opened, the guards had stopped talking to each other. They let the panel slide all the way back but still didn't walk into the room with the prisoners. Instead, they glared into the rectangular space and glanced around at each prisoner in turn, counting them like cattle in a corral.

"Where's the other one?" the head guard asked.

He was looking toward the women in the back of the room, but it was Andy who spoke up.

"What're you talking about?" Andy asked.

"The kids. There's supposed to be two of them here and I only see one. Where's the other?"

One of the women, a stout thirty-year-old with short brown hair named Beth, looked up at the guard with the same amount of distaste written on her features that she would show to a rutting pig. "They're both here," she said angrily. With that, she shifted the way she was sitting to reveal the little girl who'd been curled up in a ball between Beth and the wall.

The guard's posture eased up a bit and his lips curled

into a cruel smile. "That one thinks she can hide?"

"You scared them by barging in here like that," Beth said. "There's not even a reason for you to keep these young ones here. They can't harm a soul . . . especially not a bunch of big, tough men like yourselves."

That only served to widen the smile on the guard's face. He took a step inside and hooked his thumbs through the battered leather of his belt. "Big and tough? Yer damn right about that. Are you trying to get smart with me? Is that the smart-ass tone I heard in—"

"Shut up!" It wasn't Andy who said those words. Instead, they came from a tall, beefy deputy named Bo, who was one of the other two men locked in the rectangular room. Bo had taken a couple bullets in the hip and back, which still hadn't been enough to kill him. So far, it had been Bo's toughness keeping him alive. Unfortunately, his body was only a few steps away from being crippled.

The guard turned to him and snarled, "What the fuck? Did I just hear something from the gimp over there?"

Andy and the other man, a light-haired Virginian named Jason, got to their feet and moved to Bo's defense. They stopped before they could get too far as the rest of the guards stepped into the room. There were three of them in total, but each of the guards carried shotguns and were itching to use them.

"What d'you think you boys are gonna do?" the first guard asked. The tone in his voice was equal parts threat and challenge. Not only did they mean to scare the prisoners as they always did, but they seemed ready to pull their triggers. In fact, they *wanted* to pull them.

Andy recognized that look. It told him that he might be forced to play his cards a little sooner than he'd hoped.

TWENTY-FIVE

Andy was used to that particular guard flexing his muscles like that. Normally, however, he was kept in check by the other gunmen. This time was different. This time, the rest of the gunmen seemed to be just as ready as their leader. More than that, Andy thought he could see a few more unfamiliar faces outside the room.

That wasn't good.

Bo had managed to get to his feet and was moving forward at a slow stumble. His face was etched with determination and he fought through all the pain that accompanied each faltering step. "You're not gonna touch her," Bo said through teeth that were clenched in pain.

Lifting his shotgun so that he could aim at Bo's face, the first guard said, "Oh I'll touch her all I want. That is as soon as we're done clearing this place out of all you worthless pieces of dirt."

The women huddled closer together, turning their bodies so that they could better protect the children.

Three guards had moved into the room and fanned out to form a line. They each held their shotguns at the ready as their eyes darted back and forth between each of the three male prisoners.

Andy took half a step forward, but stopped when he saw the tense look on the closest guard's face. "Hold off here," he said in the most soothing voice he could manage. "Your boss still wants us alive."

"What makes you think that?"

"Because otherwise we would've been dead already. Am I right or wrong?"

"It don't matter which you are."

At that moment, Andy knew there would be no talking his way out of that spot. The guards were so set in their decision that their eyes seemed somewhat blank. It was as though they didn't hear anything that came from the prisoners. All they knew was what they needed to do.

They weren't the only ones. Andy knew what he needed to do as well. With a quick glance to Bo and Jason, he let them know that it was time for them all to make their move. Not only was it what they needed to do . . . it was the only thing they *could* do.

"If you want to start shooting," Andy said as he walked up closer to the nearest guard, "then you'd better start with me."

That guard narrowed his eyes and nodded once. "I got no problem with that."

Now that Clint had gotten more of a handle of the odd mind behind the town of Mason, he didn't have as many questions to ask the gunman he'd overpowered. What he mainly wanted was for the other man to fill in the pieces Clint had missed of the conversation he'd partly overheard.

Cam didn't mind saying that since he figured Clint probably had heard most of it anyway. When it came to more specific details regarding the prisoners, he was a little more hesitant to spill his guts.

"Where are they?" Clint had asked.

Cam said nothing.

Time was running out and Clint knew it wouldn't be long before he would have to fight his way through yet another batch of armed men. So to cut through the bullshit that he knew was coming, Clint used another talent he'd acquired from years spent sitting around a poker table.

He placed his palm upon the handle of his gun, stared into Cam's eyes and said, "Last chance. Start talking, or I'll send you to hell so you can sit right alongside your friend back there."

Cam's first instinct was to keep his mouth shut, if only to make Clint's life as difficult as possible. When he looked into Clint's eyes, however, he didn't see the first trace of emotion. There was no anger, deceit, or even tension. Clint's face was a blank mask, which was somehow much more unsettling than any twisted sneer.

Once that cold, unfeeling gaze seeped all the way down to Cam's gut, he couldn't speak fast enough. The gunman didn't feel scared, although he was most definitely concerned for his life. Instead, he felt that Clint was speaking the God's honest truth and would kill him in an instant if the desire happened to pass through his mind.

After spilling out locations and what details he knew, Cam was happy just to have Clint look away from him. It wasn't until that very moment that he knew what it felt like to have the hand of Death reach out for him. The jarring chill still crawled beneath his skin as Clint stepped back and peeked into the hallway.

He didn't see anyone coming, but Clint knew well enough that that didn't mean much. There could be swarms of killers lurking behind the walls like rats with guns and he wouldn't know about it until they started flowing toward him.

For the moment, he could only go by what he could sense. Ready to draw the Colt in an instant, he looked back to Cam and said, "Your belt. Take it off."

A questioning look came over Cam's face, but he did what he was told.

"Buckle it and wrap it around your wrists," Clint ordered.

The gunman did that too, all the while feeling the icy chill of that dreaded hand reaching out for him once again.

All Clint did was cinch up the belt so that Cam's hands were tied securely together. He then opened the secret door, dragged Cam over to it like a dog by a leash and then slammed the door shut.

When Clint walked away, Cam thought for a moment that he was going to be able to pounce on him when his back was turned. But the instant he started to move, he was brought to a jarring halt that nearly took him off his feet.

Looking down, Cam saw that the other end of the belt had been jammed into the door right where the locking mechanism was. With the panel so tightly closed, even when Cam tried to work the latch device, the leather strap kept the door from budging.

Cam turned to where Clint had been standing, but found that he was alone in the room.

TWENTY-SIX

Clint walked out of that room and found himself in an entirely different building. Even though he'd been expecting as much, it was still a little disconcerting to be so misplaced like that. He'd become used to a lot of things over the years, but traveling via secret corridors and hidden doorways was not one of them.

It was great to look out the window, however. The first thing he noticed was that night had already fallen, and the stars overhead were a sight that soothed his soul. But there wasn't enough time to take things in. Instead, he had a job to do and for a change he actually had a good idea of how he was going to do it.

He kept to the shadows once he left the town hall, making his way to the building that he knew held Mr. Mason's prisoners. Having gotten various bits and pieces from two different sources, Clint was fairly certain he was headed in the right direction. The more humbling part of that thought was that it was the *only* direction he had.

Clint headed toward the building that was his destination and kept walking right past the front door. He made his way around the building and into the alley alongside of it. Hoping that he hadn't been taken for a sucker, Clint felt along the wall for a dent somewhere near his hip level.

According to Cam, it wasn't going to be much more than an imperfection in the building that could have been put there by a passing wagon or careless rider bouncing off the building. Any structure that was more than a year old would have plenty such casual scars and Clint didn't have any trouble finding one at roughly the correct height.

Once there, he slid his finger into the dent and pushed.

He felt the wood give way only slightly before stopping. There was no rattle or other sound to let him know he'd hit pay dirt, but he kept on pushing while starting to lift up and out.

This time, he did get something for his troubles: a welcome rumble as a section of the wall only slightly shorter than himself moved up as though being lifted off some kind of rut that had been dug into the ground. Clint then swung the panel inward to find himself staring into a very familiar corridor. The passage looked identical to the one he'd found in the saloon except it curved sharply to the left almost immediately.

Right before he stepped into the enclosed space, Clint cursed himself for not remembering to either grab a lantern or replenish his supply of matches. He left the door open instead, chalking up the mistake in his brain so it wouldn't happen again.

There wasn't much light filtering in from the outside, but even that small amount was better than the total, tomblike blackness inside. Cam had said that the passage didn't go for too long before opening into a room where guards could sit. Clint hoped the gunman had been telling the truth about that much or else he was in for a whole lot of fumbling around in the dark.

It turned out that Clint's interrogation skills were better than he'd thought. The passage hooked sharply to the left and then only ran for another ten or fifteen feet before ending in a wall. Clint moved his fingers gently over the wall, keeping in mind all the different triggers he'd seen so far.

The grain was smooth, without a dent to be found.

There were no rough knotholes or any such designs that he could feel.

What he *could* feel, however, were a few very light imperfections along the surface of the wood near the corner where the top of the wall met the ceiling. They felt like scratches, to be precise. Three of them.

Clint put his hand upon those scratches and pushed in.

When he heard the *click*, Clint smiled like a kid who'd just found where his parents hid the Christmas presents. The panel in front of him came loose and swung out with little effort. No matter what else could be said about this Mr. Mason, he was one hell of a craftsman.

The door opened without making a sound. Clint stepped out of the darkened corridor and he immediately saw just how easy it was to blend in with the shadows once he had such good materials to work with. All he had to do was take the least amount of care in not tripping over himself and he could glide over the floor like a ghost.

The boards were practically squeak-proof and the hinges were oiled to perfection. The two men who were standing in the next room had their back to him and thanks to the well-made structure, Clint was able to sneak up on them without a hitch.

He got close enough to reach out and tap them on the shoulders. Only then did Clint feel some degree of restitution for what had happened to him in the saloon. More than that, he didn't feel so bad for letting all those men get the drop on him so easily. He barely knew his way around and he'd been able to get close enough for this.

"Excuse me?" Clint said in a casual voice. When both of the other men turned around, he asked, "Could I get some directions? I seem to be lost."

For a moment, neither of the other men knew quite

what to do. Their eyes were wide with disbelief and they froze for a second or two, each waiting for the other one to do something so he could follow.

Clint wasn't about to let them regain their senses and snapped his right fist straight into the closest man's jaw. His knuckles drove right into their target, twisting the guard's head in a quarter circle and putting out his lights quicker than a pair of wet fingers around a wick.

The second guard was starting to move, but he wasn't fast enough to avoid Clint's left, which caught him right in the solar plexus. Struggling to pull in a breath after getting the wind knocked out of him, the guard found it difficult to move right away as the force from Clint's blow rattled him all the way down to his boots.

Reaching out to grab the other man's wrist before he could get to his gun, Clint punched the guy in the face with enough force to finish the job he'd started. The guard looked as though he was going to tough it out, but then his eyes glazed over and he started wobbling from one foot to another.

Clint placed a finger on the man's head, pushed him over and moved toward the door the men had been guarding.

TWENTY-SEVEN

Having already set his mind to the task at hand, Andy didn't allow himself to think about anything else besides what he had to do. He could see the shotguns Bo and Jason pointed at him, so he didn't have to anticipate what it would feel like once those triggers were pulled. If he did that, he would only cause himself to pause. And pausing at any moment might just be the last thing he would ever do.

All the planning and talking with the other two men in the rectangular prison had led up to this moment. They all knew one or more of them might have to die for the rest of them to get their freedom. In the end, they'd all decided that dying or getting out were both better than staying where they were and waiting for the hammer to fall.

They'd thought that when they were talking and planning.

Now that it was time to make their ultimate move, they had to see if their spirits were up for more than a whole lot of hopeful talk.

Bo's jaw was set into a line of grim determination. He moved faster than he had the entire time he'd been in that room and every last step was sheer agony. That much was written all over his face, but he was still coming toward the man closest to him.

Although not quite as willing to charge as the hobbled deputy, Jason took a deep breath and stood up straight. He reminded Andy of a man standing in front of a firing line, determined and ready to face what was coming.

There was nothing else left for Andy to do but throw himself into the fire as well. After all, there wasn't going to be a better time than—

Suddenly, there was a heavy thud coming from the other side of the door, which was still propped open. It sounded like something had fallen from the ceiling or had even been dropped onto the roof. With everything sounding somewhat muffled, it was hard to tell exactly what it was. Judging by the looks on the guards' faces, the sound was every bit as much a surprise to them as it was to the prisoners.

"What the hell?" said one of the guards who was closest to the door. He turned and looked over his shoulder, straining to see down the short hallway leading to the next room.

Both of the other men started to look a little jumpy as they were forced to divide their attention between the prisoners as well as whatever was going on behind them. They stepped back and gripped their shotguns a little tighter.

At first, Andy and the other prisoners didn't quite know what to think. The men had all been ready to make their last stand and all of a sudden, the guards found something else to occupy their attention. When he looked over at Bo and Jason, he saw they were just as shocked as he was. But Andy's thoughts quickly turned to the best way to take advantage of the situation. All he had to do was nod once to them and they were all back on the right track.

To Andy's surprise, Jason was the first one of them to

move. The man from Virginia sucked in a quick breath and all but threw himself toward the closest guard. That gunman was still looking over his shoulder when Jason made contact, quickly snapping his head around when he felt the impact, which knocked him a foot or so sideways.

Andy heard the scuffle more than saw it because he was already committed to his own attack. Reaching out with both hands, he wanted to wrest the shotgun away from the man in front of him. If he got his hands on one of those weapons, he knew the break for freedom would go a whole lot smoother.

Since he'd moved a split-second after Jason, Andy wasn't able to get as much surprise as the first man. Unfortunately, moving slower than any of the others, Bo would get no amount of surprise whatsoever. That didn't stop the wounded man from doing what had to be done and he made his move using more brute force than speed since his bulk was all he really had going for him.

Once all three guards were tussling with the prisoners, the room erupted into a violent storm of noise and the pounding of feet against the floor. The rectangular room took on the quality of a battlefield where chaos was the only ruling factor.

Guards screamed for the prisoners to back away. Prisoners gnashed their teeth and pressed whatever slight advantage they might have had. All the while, all three groups were struggling for control of the things that would end the fight almost instantly: the shotguns.

One of those weapons went off, filling the room with explosive thunder and the screams of the women and children, who covered their heads in the back of the room. If anyone was hit by the blast, they either didn't know it yet or were too engrossed in their fight to stop even if they'd been hurt.

Andy had a hold of his guard's shotgun with one hand around the barrel and the other down past the trigger guard. He glared over the weapon, directly into the eyes of the guard. The only thing that came from either of their mouths was a savage, almost animal snarl.

Even when another shotgun went off behind them, they didn't take their eyes off each other. Both of them knew to do so would be to hand the other man an opening. With beads of sweat forming on their brows and muscles tensing desperately, neither one of them was going to give the other the slightest advantage to use against them. That would only mean death in a fight like that.

With that thought in mind, Andy caught a glimpse of something moving behind the guard. He didn't take his eyes away to get too good of a look, but he could definitely see a figure in the doorway leading out of the room.

It could have been another guard, but somehow Andy doubted that. Mainly, it was because of the way the figure stood and took in the whole situation rather than simply charging in and helping one of the other gunmen.

That figure stood and looked around but not for long. By the time Andy managed to pull the barrel of the shotgun out of the guard's hand, he could see that figure running through the door, headed for the spot where Bo was struggling for his life.

Andy could only pray that the figure was on their side, or Bo would be the first one to pay the ultimate price.

TWENTY-EIGHT

Clint had been worried that whoever was nearby would come running once they heard the sound of the two guards hitting the floor. After knocking both of the men out, Clint was preparing himself for reinforcement, but none seemed to be coming.

He could see another door, which he almost discounted simply because it was in plain sight. But there was a heavy latch on that door as well as brackets for a thick piece of wood to be fitted into place for extra security. Whatever was behind that door, someone wanted to keep it there, which made the possibility that he'd found the prisoners even more likely.

The question in Clint's mind regarding the possibility of reinforcements was also answered when he heard the sound of a scuffle coming from behind the other door. The latch had already been pulled back and the piece of timber was sitting next to the doorway instead of inside the brackets.

Obviously, there were more guards in that other room, since it wouldn't make sense to just leave everything unlocked like that. Clint wanted to figure as much of the situation out as possible before charging in. After all that had already happened, he felt he'd had his fill of running into things blindly.

It was at that moment when he heard a noise coming from the next room. There was more than just steps. In fact, there were voices and the sounds of a fistfight going on in there, which made Clint want to rush in and see who was beating on who.

Fighting back the urge to charge in, Clint drew his Colt and stepped through the door with all the heavy locks. Unlike the last several doors he'd stepped through, this one didn't lead into one of the compact corridors. Instead, it opened into a normal hallway that ended in a door that was just as reinforced as the one before it.

Clint noticed something else about that next door, however. It had a recessed panel where a handle should have been.

Already, Clint could see shapes of people moving back and forth in the distinctive motion of a struggle. By the sound of it, there was more than one fight going on and when Clint finally stepped into the rectangular room, he was ready to be thrown into the middle of one hell of a ruckus.

On one hand, he was right. There was more than one fight going on. But what he didn't expect was that the fight didn't seem to involve him in the slightest. Well . . . not yet, anyway.

When he could finally get a look at the entire room, Clint had to take a moment to soak it all in. In a way, it was so much easier when he was the one being jumped by an attacker. Now, coming in once the brawl had already commenced, he wasn't sure where to lend his help. A shotgun blast had already sounded, making it that much easier for Clint to slip in unnoticed and get a feel for the lay of the land.

Spotting the women huddled in the back and the general layout of the room, Clint was certain this was where

the prisoners were being kept. He then looked at the three
groups of men fighting amongst themselves and immediately spotted that each group consisted of one man trying to gain control of the shotguns held by another.
Judging by the condition of the clothes and the wounds
on some of the men, it wasn't too difficult to figure out
which ones were the prisoners and which were the guards.

The pair struggling closest to him was made up of a
lean, muscular man in a jacket and a much larger, bulkier
man who could barely keep himself upright. The healthier
of the two had already gained the advantage over the bigger one and was in the middle of raining down punch
after punch into the other man's face. Now that he knew
which side needed his help, Clint couldn't think of a better
place or time to start lending a hand.

Taking a move from the arsenal of lawman Wyatt Earp,
Clint moved up behind the guard attacking Bo and tapped
him on the shoulder. When the guard stopped to look,
Clint smashed him in the face with the handle of his Colt.
Actually, Wyatt might have done things a little differently,
since it would have been simpler to take the other man
out without warning him first. Either way, the guard was
just as unconscious no matter how it had happened.

Bo let out a shaky breath while coughing up a mouthful
of blood. "Who . . . who are you?" he asked.

"I'm here to help," Clint said while grabbing the shotgun from the fallen guard's hands. "Take this and we'll
worry about introductions later." As soon as the big man
took the gun from him, Clint turned his attention to the
next pair that were fighting no more than four or five feet
away.

That guard had also just gotten the upper hand over a
slender young man with a face that looked as though it
had nearly been beaten off his skull. When he looked up,
Jason saw Clint there and stared just long enough for the
guard to notice. Clint wasn't able to get to those two be-

fore the guard spun around and took a look for himself.

Although the guard looked surprised, he didn't let himself be distracted enough to keep from smashing Jason across the jaw with the butt of his shotgun. Jason's head snapped to one side under the force of the blow and he dropped to his knees next to the guard.

Clint saw the shotgun swinging toward him and just managed to swing his left hand out and to the side before the trigger was pulled. His forearm smacked into the shotgun barrel, knocking it away from him as fiery smoke erupted from the weapon.

Clint acted purely on instinct as he jabbed the Colt into the guard's belly and pulled the trigger. The other man let out a grunt as the muffled gunshot lifted him off his feet and blew a hole through to his back. His eyes were trained on Clint as the hand of death swept the guard up and then dropped his empty shell of a body onto the floor.

That image sank deeply into Clint's mind. Although he'd never seen the other man before and knew he was defending his life as well as the lives of several others, that didn't make what he'd done any easier to bear. Killing was still killing, no matter who it was and Clint knew he'd feel the presence of that ghost for plenty of nights to come.

Unfortunately, that ghost would have plenty of others to keep it company.

Clint choked back the feeling of those dying eyes drilling through him and looked toward the remaining prisoner who was still fighting for his life.

TWENTY-NINE

Even though he was more than a little distracted by the guard trying to kill him by either beating him to death or shooting him with the shotgun, Andy couldn't help but notice what the newest arrival was doing. In fact, it was hard to miss the fact that not just one, but two of the other guards had already been taken out thanks to that stranger.

Andy was quickly brought back to his own battle when he felt a fist drive into his gut. The guard's knuckles were so hard that they might have been forged from iron. All of Andy's breath came rushing out of his lungs until the edges of his vision began to blur. Even so, he refused to let go of the end of the shotgun he'd managed to take from the other man.

That first punch was followed by another, driving even deeper into the same spot. Despite all the strength and desperate energy he pulled up, Andy was unable to keep on his feet after being hit that second time. An icy wave of pain soaked through him, weighing him down until even the sounds inside the room were having a hard time reaching him.

After dropping down to one knee, Andy noticed something moving along the floor. It approached from behind

119

the guard like a puddle of ink that had been spilled onto
the ground. It was a shadow and it belonged to the
stranger.

The guard had noticed the other man approaching him
as well and immediately spun around to bring the shotgun
to bear on him. His thumb snapped back both of the hammers and he was ready to fire when suddenly his target
was no longer there.

The stranger moved like a flicker of lightning, dodging
to one side while reaching for his gun belt with both
hands. Dropping down onto the floor, the stranger tossed
himself into a sideways roll while locking eyes with
Andy.

When he extended his arms again, the stranger was
holding a gun in each hand. One of the guns was held
close to the stranger's body as he entered the roll, while
the other gun was tossed through the air with a snapping
motion of his wrist.

The shotgun blasted through the air, washing out every
other sound inside the room and leaving a shrill ringing
in Andy's ears. But Andy hardly noticed anything except
for the pistol, which was sailing through the air like a gift
from God. He caught the weapon and slipped his finger
around the trigger, feeling for the first time that he actually had a chance to make it out of that room alive.

The stranger's side hit the floor and he was immediately
rolling to one side. Somehow, he managed to squeeze off
a round, which actually managed to punch a hole through
the guard's shoulder.

Seeing that, Andy was amazed that the stranger had
pulled off the maneuver while hitting his target at all. He
thanked the stranger by taking aim and firing as the guard
was spun around by the first bullet until he was facing
Andy head-on.

Andy couldn't keep the victorious smile off his face as
he pulled his trigger and sent a bullet straight through the

guard's skull. The point-blank shot sent the guard flying once again, this time straight back until his spine slapped against the hardwood floor.

The stranger kept rolling until he could extend one leg and stop himself with his foot against the wall. Doing so allowed him to get out of the way as the guard's last dying twitch pulled his second trigger and sent a spray of shotgun fire into the room.

Still laying on the ground, the stranger plucked another gun from his belt and sent it flying through the air. This time, he wasn't aiming toward Andy, but toward Jason, who was just managing to climb back up to his feet. Although the Virginia man looked stunned by what had happened, he was more than ready to take the weapon that was sailing his way.

Even before Jason could get a proper grip on his gun, the stranger was up and on his feet, walking toward Andy and looking around the room with crisp, alert eyes.

"How many more?" the stranger asked.

Andy blinked once and then said, "Guards? I don't know."

"No. Prisoners. How many more of you are there?"

"There's just us, I think. I'm not sure though."

Jason was helping Bo up to his feet and turned to shout over his shoulder. "I never heard anyone mention no more prisoners. And I listened to every last thing I could against this here wall."

"Who are you?" Andy asked.

"I'm Clint Adams."

"Thank y—"

"Don't thank me yet," Clint interrupted. "We need to get ready for some more company."

Already, the sound of more feet pounding against the floor could be heard coming from the next room.

THIRTY

Alonzo Mason stood in what had once been West Bend's general store. It was now his own personal storage shed since he'd claimed everything inside of it for himself. The reason he was there was so he could keep tabs on what was going on inside his town. With all the shooting that had erupted, there was no better place to do just that since the store was right across the street from the old Town Hall.

For a man who'd grown accustomed to such complete silence, as was the norm in the town, Mason could detect just about anything that broke that silence. By the time the gunshots had made it through the walls of the other building and into the street, they were nothing more than rumbles in the air. Mason closed his eyes and soaked in those leftover rumbles, savoring them like a connoisseur of fine wine.

The gunshots had stopped for a little while and then erupted like a storm for a few prolonged bursts. After that, the streets had gone back to the deathly silence that was the norm. After that, Mason replayed the noises inside his head a few more times, doing his best to put pictures to the sounds.

He smiled at the distinctive roar of shotguns, but didn't seem too pleased with the popping crackles of pistol fire. And he didn't seem to respond at all to the much louder thump of footsteps approaching from behind.

Even though he didn't see any reaction from Mason, the man who was walking up to him stopped and waited. He knew damn well that his presence had been detected. It simply wasn't his time to speak just yet. Right as he was about to clear his throat or make some other kind of noise to announce himself, he saw Mason turn slowly around to face him.

"Tell me, Luke," Mason said to his most valued gun hand. "Tell me what happened in there, because I wasn't supposed to hear gunshots coming from that building for a while yet."

Luke didn't allow himself to be taken in by the calmness in Mason's tone. Instead, he kept his back straight and his eyes averted slightly, just as he'd been commanded when the town had fallen into Mason's hands. "Some of the men went after the prisoners," he said.

"And did you know this was going to happen?"

Pausing for a second, Luke nodded. "Yeah. I heard some things."

"And why didn't you tell me about these things. Aren't I the one who's supposed to know everything that happens in this town? Aren't I the one who needs to know everything?"

"Yes, sir."

"I can't just know everything, Luke." Relaxing his posture just a little bit, Mason walked past the other man and headed down one of the store's two aisles on his way to the back. "Everyone else might think I know everything and I do know just about all there is to know inside this town, but I need to rely on my most trusted associates to tell me the things I don't know."

"I understand, sir."

"The men, for example. They're your responsibility."

Luke nodded again.

Stopping with his hands folded behind his back, Mason spun on the balls of his feet until he was staring into Luke's eyes. "If you can't uphold your responsibilities, why else should I keep you around?"

"I can do my job." This time, Luke was unable to keep the anger and frustration out of his voice. His lips were drawn tightly over his teeth, lending a rasping sound to his words. "I can't tell you every . . . single . . . thing that I hear. Most of it is just bellyaching and gossip. The men want to make their move across the state line. You know that. I told you that."

"But you never told me they had something against my prisoners."

"Those prisoners are too dangerous to keep. The men know you don't want to ransom them and they know you don't want to let them go." Breaking a well-known rule, Luke looked up and returned Mason's stare. "That makes those prisoners the only thing keeping us here when we could be moving on to—"

"To where?" Mason spat. "Hmm? Where would you go without me to lead you? Would you rather become just a bunch of traveling thieves robbing stagecoaches and getting shot down by some snot-nosed posse? Or would you rather stay with me and sink your teeth into entire towns like we did this one?"

"They want to stay with you," Luke answered, fighting back the urge to grab the broad-shouldered man by the front of his shirt and start shaking. "Otherwise, they would have ganged up on you by now and buried you six feet under."

Mason didn't so much as twitch at that. He didn't even blink. "And would you have led them against me?"

Although Luke didn't answer, he didn't look away either.

The silence from the rest of the town seeped through the walls to infect the old store like a stifling fog. Neither man moved for a few seconds, although it seemed like hours before Luke finally broke the morbid stillness.

"If you wanted us to stay in this place for the rest of our lives like a bunch of rats, then yes, I would have led them against you."

Mason's eyes narrowed and he let out a breath that resembled the whisper of air that came out when a tomb was broken open after years of being sealed. His lips parted as if to speak, but his eyes started twitching ever so slightly until he settled on what he wanted to say.

"You know," Mason finally said, "honesty in some people is very refreshing. If that answer had come out of anyone else's mouth, they would have been holding their own balls in a marble sack by morning." He reached out and slapped Luke on the shoulder. "But you get to hang onto yours for a while."

Luke nodded slowly, unsure as to what the other man was going to do. There was really no way to predict Alonzo Mason, so he'd given up a long time ago.

THIRTY-ONE

"I'm not sure if your men's plan worked, however," Mason said. "I distinctly heard a gunfight, not just gunshots."

"That's what I wanted to tell you, sir. There was a fight and mostly because of one man who was in that fight."

"What are you talking about?"

"The man who got away from the ambush in the saloon," Luke said. "That's what I'm talking about. It's because of him that there was something more than a slaughter when the rest of my men went down to remove those prisoners from the picture. He's tipping the scales in the wrong direction everywhere he goes."

"Oh, is he? And why is that?"

"Hell if I know. Whoever he is, he's not only taken out nearly half a dozen of our men, but he's figured out a way to use the tunnels while he does it."

That, quite obviously, didn't sit well at all with Mason. His gaze focused into an intense beam like sunlight passing through a magnifying glass to burn whatever helpless ants were nearby. When he blinked, some of the intensity had dissipated, but not very much. "He knows about my tunnels?"

"One of the boys in the saloon told him."

"Which one?"

"It doesn't matter," Luke said. "He was wounded when I found him. He was dead a couple seconds after he told me everything he'd done."

Mason nodded. "Good. So this situation with the prisoners, does it have anything to do with this new arrival?"

"I wish it did. The men want to get the prisoners out of the way so we can move on. They think those folks are the only things still keeping us all here. That stranger just happened to stumble upon those men when they'd already started to clean those prisoners out."

"And?"

Luke pulled in a deep breath and let it out like a snarl in the back of his throat. "The prisoners put up a fight, but it wasn't until the stranger came by that the odds really shifted against my men. Once that happened, every one of those men who went into that holding cell were killed."

Although there was plenty going on inside Alonzo Mason's head, the only thing that showed was the motion of his jaw as it slid back and forth, grinding his teeth together. "So you were there?" he asked, shifting his gaze so he could look directly at Luke. "That's how you know all of this, right? Because you were there at some point?"

"Yeah, I was there, but it wasn't until everything was over. The stranger came in through the alley entrance to the old Town Hall and only knocked out the two guards posted outside the prisoners' room. They were all gone by the time I got there. The rest of my men were dead.

"Going by what one of those men told me, another bunch of my men came in to see what was keeping the first three. When that happened, the prisoners were ready. They must've taken the shotguns from the others and when more came after them, they blew them apart as soon as they ran into the room."

Mason shook his head and turned back around so that

he was facing the back wall. "But that other man was still
alive to tell you this."

"That's right. He didn't say anything about it, but I'm
thinking he played possum when the prisoners came out
of there."

"Did you take care of him as well?" Mason asked.
"This other guard who laid there while my prisoners got
away?"

"No, sir. I didn't."

"Good. Self-preservation can't be mixed up with cow-
ardice. Besides, it seems I might be quickly running out
of men if this keeps up much longer."

"That's what I was thinking."

Mason reached out with his left hand and placed it
against a spot on the wall that wasn't marked or damaged
in any way. He simply put his hand there and left it as
though he thought he might need to support his weight
against something. "You know what I'm thinking right
now, Luke?"

The other man had wondered that very thing on so
many occasions that he couldn't even count them all. In
that period of time, he'd formed some opinions and come
up with a couple ideas of his own, but none of them
seemed to cover every angle or explain everything he'd
seen reflected with his boss's eyes. Rather than open up
that particular can of worms, Luke simply said, "No, sir."
And that was the God's honest truth.

"I'm thinking that we could use a man like this one.
I'm thinking that maybe him coming here wasn't an ac-
cident, but some kind of gift handed to me by fate. You
believe in fate?"

"No."

"Well, a man in my position has to believe in fate to
some degree or other. And even with the cuts in my group
made by this stranger, having a man as dangerous as that
working for me could more than make up for it. In fact,

with a smaller, stronger force to work with, we won't even need those prisoners."

Luke thought that was a good thing for Mason to think. Especially since not only were those prisoners long gone, but even he wouldn't miss them.

"See what else you can find about this man," Mason continued. "I want to know where he is and what else he knows about this town. When you find him, bring him to me."

Even though he didn't want to ask the question, Luke figured it was bound to come up sooner or later, so it was best to just get it out of the way. "What if I find the prisoners?"

Mason was silent for a few moments and then nodded sharply once to himself. "Forget about them. They're too much trouble. If you find them finish the job your men started. It's for the best." When he said that last part, Mason sounded as though the whole thing involving the prisoners' execution had been his idea.

Luke didn't give a damn what Mason thought on the subject anymore. "I'll get right on it," he said, with renewed vigor.

"Do that first," Mason said. "I'll start working on meeting this stranger myself. You can lend your hand once I've laid the groundwork."

"Yes, sir."

THIRTY-TWO

Clint and the others stormed out of the old Town Hall like an army set to sack the town. Most of them were armed and they all moved with the determination of rampaging bulls.

There had been reinforcements coming after Clint and the other three prisoners had taken down the first set of guards, but the next wave of killers were in too much of a hurry to be stealthy. Since everyone inside the rectangular room had heard the next ones coming, they greeted the gunmen with a barrage of pistol and shotgun fire that cut through those guards in a matter of seconds.

Clint hadn't even needed to fire his Colt. The three men who'd been held captive for so long were more than ready to use the weapons they'd been given against their captors. Having bought themselves some time, Clint and the other three gathered up the women and children and started heading for the door.

Now, with the open air rushing in through the secret door that Clint had left open, the entire group surged into the alley and stopped before going into the street. Clint was in the lead but he wasn't sure exactly what to expect once they all got out there. He was more surprised that there was nobody waiting for them than if there had been a firing squad assembled near the exit.

As the prisoners came out, Clint made sure they all stayed together as he constantly kept watch on what was going on around them. Even after they were all out and the door was closed behind them, the town seemed just as deserted as when Clint had first arrived.

"What do we do now?" It was Beth who asked that question. The stout woman still carried the little girl in her arms and had a fiercely protective look in her eyes.

"All of you need to get out of this place," Clint said. "You need to put this town behind you as quickly as possible and get somewhere safe."

"My folks own a spread near Carter's Bluff," Jason said. "That's no more than a day's ride from here."

Clint felt the hairs stand up on the back of his neck. They were sitting still for too long and his instincts were screaming for him to get moving. "Anywhere closer than that? Any town will do as long as there's someplace for you to rest and get out of the open."

Grunting as he stepped forward on legs that throbbed with pain, Bo nodded and said, "I was part of a posse when I . . . came here." His breathing was strained and every word was a test of his strength. "We had a place . . . we used for . . . resting and watering the horses on long rides. It's got . . . everything we need. There's some food kept there and . . . places to sleep."

The other woman, Sherryl, took hold of Bo's arm and made him put some of his weight upon her. "That sounds good," she said.

Clint nodded. "Yeah, it does. How far away is it?"

"We could get there in a few hours. Even . . . if we had to walk." When he said that last word, Bo's frame seemed to shrink down a little bit and his eyes dropped down to look at the ground. "Leave me here," he said. "I'll just . . . slow you down."

"Nobody's getting left behind," Andy said. Turning to Clint, he asked, "Isn't that right?"

But Clint was already stepping out to look down the street. After poking his head out of the alley, he glanced in the direction of the saloon. What he saw not only put a smile on his face, but surprised him. He stepped back into the alley and said, "That's exactly right. Nobody's getting left behind. And you," he said, pointing to Bo, "don't even have to walk more than half a block or so."

Bo looked hopeful, but only hesitantly so. "What?"

"I left my horse tied in front of the saloon," Clint explained. "And I'll be damned if it isn't still there."

Although he looked hopeful as well, Andy gritted his teeth and slowly shook his head. "If that's true, then won't anyone looking for you be watching that horse?"

"Probably," Clint said. "But I don't think we have much of a choice. It would be a whole lot more dangerous if we stick around here looking for wherever these guys keep their horses. Unless one of you knows?"

Clint looked from face to face, but didn't see the first indication that any of the prisoners knew where the gunmen kept their stable. "All right, then. We go with my plan. Although . . ." Suddenly, Clint stopped what he was saying as something that had already been said fit in like a puzzle piece with what he'd already been thinking.

As much as he wanted to get the prisoners out of town as quickly as possible, he didn't like the thought of having even some of them walking. The gunmen would certainly have their own horses and if they got so much as a hint of which way the prisoners had gone, it would be a simple matter of outrunning them and picking them off.

Even if Clint was to go along with them, he was uncomfortable with gambling on whether or not he could take on all of the gunmen who came out without getting even one of the prisoners hurt in the process. Then again, there might just be another way. It would still be a gamble, but not as big a one as before. And with this gamble, Clint was much more certain of coming out a winner.

He looked at the women and then focused his attention on Sherryl. "Have you ever used a gun before?" Clint asked.

She pulled a strand of her dirty blonde hair over her ear and smirked proudly. "Not until a couple minutes ago, when I dropped one of them guards on my own."

"What I'm thinking may be dangerous, but if—"

"But if I don't do something soon to help," she interrupted, "I'll never forgive myself."

Clint walked up to her. "Do you think you might be able to defend yourself again if you had to?"

Reaching into a pocket within her skirts, she produced one of the same pistols that Clint had taken from the two guards upon entering the old Town Hall. Sherryl snapped back the hammer with her thumb and then released it before pocketing the gun once again. "I think I can manage."

"Good. I want the rest of you to find a place to hide."

"I know someplace," Andy said. "They might not think to look there for a while. Especially if they're distracted."

"Even better." Looking over to the woman, Clint said, "Let's go."

THIRTY-THREE

Luke walked out of the store and stood on the worn-out boardwalk for a couple seconds. He took some time to pull in a breath of air and clear his head. After spending so much time cooped up in one of Mason's rat holes or one of the buildings that were about to fall down, being outside held a special kind of appeal.

Besides being able to simply feel wind on his face or see the sky over his head, Luke felt like he could more easily remember what it was like to be working on his own. Mason had plenty of good ideas and some of them were just crazy enough to work. But going along with the man meant bowing down to him at times, just to feed the ego that drove him to such heights.

Luke didn't allow himself to stand by for too long before setting himself to the task at hand. There was still an intruder making his way through town. He knew that much because the fine-looking stallion was still tied to the post outside the saloon. As he thought about that, Luke's eyes drifted down the street in that direction.

The first thing he saw was the shape of the horse waiting patiently right where the stranger had left it. Luke knew that some of the other men were thinking about

taking that horse for themselves, but those men weren't
entertaining those ideas any longer. They were too dead
to do much in the way of thinking.

But Luke also saw something else when he looked toward the saloon. In fact he saw two somethings making
their way toward the saloon by running in and out of the
shadows that lined the street.

The sun was long gone and the darkness was getting
thicker by the moment, but Luke was still able to make
out the shapes of two people closing in on that horse. He
squinted in the night and could tell that one of the figures
was obviously a woman. The other was a man who moved
with speed and agility without making more than a slight
rustle of sound. If he hadn't been so used to quiet darkness, Luke might not have even noticed the two figures
were there.

Moving slowly until the figures were far enough along,
Luke stepped off the boardwalk and crept behind the pair.
Just as he'd suspected, they went straight to that horse.
The man hopped into the saddle and gave the animal a
familiar pat on the neck before reaching a hand down to
help the woman up behind him.

Luke smiled to himself as he started moving faster. He
waited until the reins had been untied from the saloon's
hitching post before breaking into a run down the street.
The pair in front of the saloon had steered the horse toward the edge of town and started riding that way by the
time Luke reached the window of what had once been a
blacksmith's shop.

He didn't even get a chance to look inside before the
two barn doors leading to the forge slid open. The men
whom he'd posted there were already on their own horses
and moving out of the large, open area where the West
Bend smithy had done his work.

Luke had posted those men there to watch and be ready
in case the intruder tried to leave town. If they'd shown

up any later, he might have just put a bullet in both of their heads and considered himself better off. "What took you so long?" he snarled to the men.

"We saw you following there behind them and thought you wouldn't want us tipping them other two off."

The second of the men on horseback spoke in an excited flurry of words. "That woman was one of the prisoners, Luke. You think the others are making a run for it, too?"

"Just go after that horse and bring her back. After what happened at the old Town Hall, I doubt the rest will leave one of their own behind. Bring her back here and be quick about it."

That was all one of the gunmen had to hear before he snapped his reins and took off at a full gallop after Eclipse.

"What about you?" the remaining gunman asked. "Are you coming, too?"

Luke knew damn well that his orders were to go after the prisoners. And since one of those prisoners had been right there for him to see, he also knew Mason would want him to go after that woman and drag her back into town.

He also knew that the other man on that horse was almost certainly the intruder who had been kicking up so much hell since his arrival. Seeing the way he'd moved as well as the way the horse responded to him had convinced Luke of that much.

Even knowing all of that, Luke shook his head once and said, "No. You go on and get them two. I'm sure you can handle it on your own."

The man on horseback straightened up, looking a lot like a boy who'd just been sent to the head of the class. "Sure thing," was all he said before digging his heels into his horse and taking off like a ball from a cannon down the street.

Luke watched him go, more than a little upset that it had been so easy to deceive the other man. Then again, with that caliber of help, it made him feel a lot better about sending him off on what he suspected was a fool's errand.

All three horses couldn't even be heard within a few more seconds, which was when Luke ducked into one of the thicker shadows alongside the blacksmith's place. In his head, he counted off how many of his men had been taken out one way or another over the last couple of hours. He was left with the two on horseback and another that was hardly worth mentioning, but it might still be enough.

Knowing he had a little bit of time since the stranger was still headed out of town, Luke kept his steps light and snuck to the chapel, which was slightly west of the center of town. He wasn't much of a praying men, but the steeple in that building was the highest point around and was used as a scouting tower now that Mr. Mason was in charge.

Luke made it to the empty church in a few minutes and quickly climbed to the spot inside the place where a bell had hung when the town of West Bend used to gather for Sunday services. Once there, Luke got comfortable and spotted the points of dust being kicked up, which marked the progress of the racing horses.

Once he had that, he scanned the streets for six more figures huddled in the dark and found them about ten minutes later.

THIRTY-FOUR

Clint steered Eclipse toward the edge of town and let the Darley Arabian go as fast as it could. Behind him, Sherryl hung on almost tight enough to squeeze the breath out of him, but he didn't blame her since Eclipse was working off all the energy he'd been saving.

The wind blew over them and the ground flew beneath their feet. The farther Clint got away from the seemingly abandoned town, the more he wanted to keep going. But there were still some things he had to take care of before that could happen.

Sherryl looked over her shoulder and then immediately started tapping Clint's. "There's someone behind us!" she said, shouting to be heard over the tumultuous mixture of wind and the beating of hooves.

"How many?" Clint asked.

She looked back again just to be sure and then replied, "Looks like two. They're both on horses."

Clint took a quick look back to confirm the number and spotted both riders coming up on them from behind. Either there were fewer men in that town than he thought, or they had other ways of getting around outside the town as well.

"Damn," Clint said. "I was expecting there to be a few more."

Clint could feel the tension in Sherryl's body as she hung onto him even tighter for a moment or two. He seemed to get control of her fear, however, and loosened up enough so he could breathe. To calm her nerves a bit, Clint pulled back on the reins and slowed Eclipse to a trot.

"Two should be plenty, though," he told her. "Are you ready for this?"

Swallowing hard, she blinked her eyes and nodded once. "As ready as I'll ever be."

"Good. Because they're going to be coming up on us any second now."

Clint didn't even have to say that, since the sound of approaching hooves could already be heard. They got louder as the riders got closer, until finally two distinct shapes could be made out against the backdrop of stars and the town's silhouette.

When he spotted a cluster of trees, Clint steered Eclipse toward them and brought the stallion to a stop. He dropped down from the saddle and then reached up to help Sherryl. Although she seemed to know her way around a horse, she was nervous enough to need him to keep her from slipping.

Once she got her feet on the ground, she seemed to draw some more strength from whatever well had already gotten her that far. She lifted up her chin and looked at Clint with wide, yet surprisingly clear eyes.

"Are you still ready for this?" he asked.

"Yes. I just don't know how long I can stay ready."

"If that's your only worry, than you're in good shape. Get on over behind those trees because they're going to be here any second now."

Sherryl gathered her skirts in one hand and held them up off the ground just high enough for her to speed toward

the spot Clint had mentioned. Once she got herself positioned behind a couple thick trunks, she drew her pistol
and cocked it.

The other two horses were coming a little slower, but
they were still gaining ground quick enough. Clint led
Eclipse a little ways off the path and gave the stallion a
light slap on the rump. "Go on, boy. You'd best give us
a little room for this."

Not hurried in the slightest, Eclipse snuffed through his
nostrils and walked off the path. The Darley Arabian
found a suitable spot no more than ten or fifteen yards
away and began gnawing on some grass.

Clint kept his eyes on the trail and started backpedaling
toward the trees where Sherryl was waiting. Within thirty
seconds, he saw the pair of riders come down the path.
Before they spotted him, Clint turned and started running
toward another stand of trees.

"Hold it right there!" came a voice from the trail behind
Clint. "We see you and can shoot you down if you take
one more step!"

Clint froze and slowly raised his hands.

"Turn around."

When he did, Clint saw there were indeed only two
riders. He didn't allow the disappointment to show on his
face.

Both of the riders had their guns out and aimed at Clint.
Although it was too dark to see too many details on their
faces, the smug grins they wore would have shone
through the densest fog.

One of the riders came a few steps closer than the other.
He held a pistol in his right hand, using his left arm to
steady it. The man behind him sighted down the barrel of
a Spencer rifle. Apparently, the man with the pistol had
been elected the spokesman. "Where's the prisoner?" he
asked.

Draining every bit of intelligence from his features,

Clint looked around as though he'd suddenly forgotten where he was. "Prisoner? What prisoner?"

"We saw you had a woman with you. Where is she?"

He couldn't see Sherryl from where he was standing, but Clint could practically feel the tension coming off of her as though it was a tangible wave of heat. "I let her go a mile back," Clint said, inserting just enough of a waver in his voice to achieve just the right amount of unsteadiness.

"You're lying," the rider said.

Clint moved slowly and began shifting from foot to foot. Just when he felt that the rider was going to say something else, he let himself be seen glancing toward a nearby stand of trees. Of course, it was a clump of trees on the opposite side of the trail than where Sherryl was hiding.

Picking up on Clint's glance immediately, the rider looked over to that stand of trees and began grinning widely. "Cover him," he said while swinging down out of the saddle. "I think that bitch is a lot closer than he's lettin' on."

The rider kept his pistol trained on Clint while starting to walk over to those trees. Suddenly, there was a crackling sound coming from the spot that Clint had been trying to keep out of the gunmen's notice. The rider stopped where he was and snapped his fingers.

"Check that out," he ordered the second rider.

The instant those words came out of his mouth, the crackle of small feet upon loose leaves became a rush and both riders went on the offensive. The man with the rifle landed heavily as he dropped down off his horse, levering a round into the breach of his weapon. The one with the pistol spat out a garbled obscenity and stared at Clint with a murderous gaze.

Clint's first impulse was to drop the man directly in front of him. But the moment Sherryl had climbed onto

the saddle behind him, he'd made protecting her his number one priority. For that reason, Clint stood his ground
and shifted his aim away from the man who was firing at
him.

The Colt barked loudly in the night, spitting a piece of
hot lead through the air, past the closest man's head, and
into the rifleman's right temple. The bullet entered with a
wet slapping noise, knocking the rifleman off his feet. He
was dead before he hit the ground.

Feeling the bullet whip past his face was enough to
make the other gunman pause for a second as his body
tensed up for a second. When he saw that he was still
alive, he wasted no time in aiming his gun and squeezing
the trigger.

Just as his hammer was about to fall, another pistol
sounded off. The blast didn't come from Clint, but instead
came from the trees where the rifleman had been headed.
The man with the pistol figured out that much before a
bullet dug a deep trench through the front of his chest.
The pain caused him to straighten up and the next bullet
punched a hole through his lung.

Clint stood there, ready to fire at the closer of the two
gunmen, but finding it suddenly unnecessary. He looked
around as Sherryl came walking out from the trees.

"I thought that man was going to kill you," she said.

"I was just going to say the same thing to you. Thanks
for covering me."

"I know that it wasn't part of the plan."

"That's all right. I think I can let it slide this one time."

THIRTY-FIVE

Clint rode Eclipse back to town almost as fast as the stallion could carry him. The only reason he didn't let the Darley Arabian go full-out was because he couldn't let Sherryl fall too far behind.

After taking out the two gunmen who'd followed them, Clint had waited to see if any more were still on their trail. When no more came, he and Sherryl gathered up the two gunmen's horses and led them back to town.

All three horses stopped at the edge of town, where Clint climbed down from the saddle. He didn't have to walk ten feet before he could see several other shapes moving toward him in the darkness. He waited with his hand hovering over his Colt, but soon he could see that the other shapes were the rest of the prisoners, led by Andy.

"Where's Bo?" Clint asked.

The hobbling man was moving much slower than the rest, but refused to let any of the others stay behind to help him. And despite all those constant refusals, Beth remained attached to his side so she could be his support.

"We heard shooting," Andy said.

"Not only did we get another of those two guards,"

Sherryl said excitedly, "but we got their horses."

Clint helped Jason and the two children climb onto the back of a brown Dunn, which had been owned by the rifleman. "You'll be able to travel a lot faster this way."

Andy stood in front of Clint and looked stunned. "I don't know how to thank you."

"You can thank me by telling me where this cabin is that you'll be going to so I can find you. And you can also make sure nothing happens to Eclipse along the way."

"Eclipse?" Just then, Andy noticed how Clint was patting the Darley Arabian stallion when he'd mentioned that name. "But that's your horse. You can't just—"

"All of you can't get out of here on two horses. Besides, the big man there's been through a lot. He deserves to ride the best." What Clint didn't want to say was that he figured Eclipse was the only horse of the three that could carry Bo as well as someone else and still travel with any amount of speed.

"We don't have enough time to argue," Clint said. "You've all got to get moving before any more of those hired guns come after you."

Bo walked up to Eclipse, took one look at him and shook his head. "We can't take your horse. How are you gonna meet us without a horse to ride on?"

"I'll find a way. Now just go."

"But this is too good an animal and you've done so much already. I couldn't possibly—"

"I'm not giving him to you forever," Clint said in a hasty tone. "Just letting you borrow him so you can get out of here alive and I can clear my conscience. Now, the longer you stay, the more likely it is I'll have to save your sorry butt one more time."

It looked like Bo was about to say something else, but Clint stopped him with a quickly raised index finger. "Stop right there. If you make me lift you onto that saddle, you'll be responsible for breaking my back as well. Can you live with that?"

Finally, Bo shook his head and smiled. "No. I suppose not. Thanks a lot, Clint. I appreciate it. We all do."

One by one, the prisoners said a quick good-bye to Clint as they all climbed onto their horses. Sherryl had slid down from her saddle and rushed over to him, wrapping her arms around Clint's neck.

"Thank you so much," she said before kissing him on the lips.

As much as he wanted to prolong the moment, Clint lifted Sherryl back onto her horse and stepped back. Bo gave him directions on how to get to the cabin where they were all headed and shook Clint's hand one more time.

Clint watched as the horses were all turned and riding away from town. Eclipse hung back for longer than the rest, turning around to look at Clint with a slightly confused stare. He made a shooing gesture with both hands, which didn't do a bit of good.

Running over to the Darley Arabian, he patted the horse on the neck and said, "It's all right. Go on and I'll be back for you."

He didn't really think the stallion understood the words, but Eclipse seemed to catch on to the meaning well enough. Letting out a labored breath, he accepted Bo's direction and walked away. Clint watched and made a promise to himself that he would finish his business and join up with Eclipse as quickly as possible.

THIRTY-SIX

Luke watched from the steeple atop the church as all the figures gathered just outside of town. He'd spotted those prisoners skulking around like they thought they were truly fooling anyone ever since the first two had ridden away. At that point in the game, he was just as happy to be rid of those prisoners by any means necessary.

Even though Mason had seemed to come around toward the end of their last conversation, Luke didn't kid himself that things were going to change for the better. Mason wasn't the type to let something go so easily. Although he didn't know what the other man had planned, Luke was just glad to have those prisoners out of his sight. He was even more glad to see that one figure didn't leave with all the rest.

He'd figured that the stranger wouldn't just up and leave. It was a feeling in his gut as though he felt some kind of strange kinship with the man who'd taken such a massive bite out of Mason's little operation. Luke simply knew that a fighting man like that wouldn't cut out before the entire job was done.

Sure enough, Luke grinned to himself when he saw that solitary figure turn around and head back to town while

146

all the others steered their horses in the opposite direction. This thing wasn't over yet. Not for Luke, anyway. As one fighting man to another, there was an unspoken debt between them that had to be paid. It would have gone against both men's natures to leave such a thing hanging.

His business in the watchtower completed, Luke climbed down and walked through the main room of the chapel. Dusty pews lined up in front of an abandoned altar greeted him when he entered. Sitting in the front pew was another solitary figure. This one was a lot different than the one he'd seen from up above.

This figure was much trimmer, much curvier, and much more comfortable stretched out in the dark like some reclining cat.

"Hello, Paula," Luke said as he walked past the altar. "How long've you been waiting there?"

"Not long. I thought you might like to know that the stranger's name is Clint Adams."

The name struck a chord inside Luke's mind. He recognized it, but somehow wasn't surprised to hear it in connection with that particular intruder. It just seemed to fit in with everything he'd seen the other man do and with the way he'd been handling himself.

"You know who that is, right?" Paula asked.

"Yes. I know who that is. I might've been disappointed if I knew that so many of my men were taken down by someone other than a man like that. My men were good, but they weren't his caliber."

"You think he was sent?"

"By the law? No. By something else, maybe."

Paula smirked and got to her feet. She walked over and stood next to Luke, who was glancing toward the wooden crucifix that had been nailed to the wall behind the altar. "Are you becoming a religious man all of a sudden?"

A stunted laugh made Luke's shoulders jump a bit before the sound got stuck in his throat. "Not hardly. But if anyone deserves to get knocked off his pedestal by fate or whatever there is it's our lord and master Alonzo Mason or whatever he's calling himself today."

"Mason's done a lot for us. You can't deny that."

"He sure has done a lot. One of the things he's done is make us stay here long enough for us to gather a bunch of innocent people for no good reason until they was found by someone strong enough to take them away. He's also gotten damn near all of us killed. Something like this was bound to happen sooner or later. You've got to know that."

After a long, silent pause, she let out a breath and said, "I know. But that doesn't mean that we have to just roll over and let this Clint Adams put us away. I've got too much invested in this to give it up so easily. Besides, now that those prisoners are gone . . . we can move across the state line that much sooner."

"I like the way you think. But we've still got to deal with Adams. He's coming back, you know."

"I know. And since he's looking for someone to save . . ." Turning and heading toward the door, Paula ran her fingers through her thick, dark hair and mussed it up. "I aim to make sure he gets what he's after."

THIRTY-SEVEN

As Clint walked back into town, he wanted to start firing shots in the air, pounding his fists against the run-down buildings or even let out a holler just to flush out however many rats were still waiting in the nest. He knew he was probably still outnumbered and certainly didn't know all of the secrets beneath the town's dusty facade, so he fought back those initial urges.

He was tired.

He was hungry.

And he was sick of finding his way through the entire town in much the same way he'd groped his way in the dark while trying to navigate some of those passages.

But underneath all of the frustration, he also knew he couldn't just leave the place. There could still be more prisoners hidden somewhere, just like there could be more killers hiding in the shadows. He knew for certain that Mr. Mason was still around somewhere and Clint wasn't about to leave the party until he'd had a chance to thank his host personally.

Clint moved into one of the nearby shadows between two of the buildings he was about to pass. The night was full of starlight, which was complimented by a dull, pale glow cast from the mood overhead. Three-quarters of the luminous sphere could be seen, making the empty streets and quiet buildings seem even more ghostly.

Stopping to look around, Clint found a small house situated away from the main row of buildings not too far away. He circled it once, getting a feel for the size of the building. Once that was done, he dropped down to his hands and knees so he could look under the rickety porch. As far as he could tell, there was nothing beneath the building to connect it to any kind of tunnel. There wasn't even a cellar.

The back door was open and there didn't seem to be much inside the place except for a few spare pieces of furniture and various other odds and ends scattered about. Clint walked around the house, looking through what had been left behind by its previous owners while comparing the dimensions to the ones he'd taken on the outside.

Both sets of measurements were close enough to equal that Clint figured there couldn't be much by way of tunnels or secret rooms along the outer walls. The walls inside were thin and decrepit enough for him to be certain that there were no surprises there either.

It made him feel some degree of comfort knowing that the rats weren't able to dig their nests into every last nook and cranny after all. When Clint was done with his walking, he settled into a room in the corner of the building that looked out onto the rest. That way, he could feel that he wasn't as likely to get attacked from out of nowhere. Plus, there were windows on both of the outside walls, which meant he was sure there were no passages in those walls either.

The room had obviously been a bedroom. There were spots on the floor and imprints in the dust where a dresser and wardrobe had been. Mostly, however, it was the collapsed bed that gave it away. The bed was nice, but the frame was cracked and the mattress was ripped open and spilling its fluffy guts onto the floor. Something like that wouldn't have been worth the effort of packing into a wagon.

Clint lowered himself onto the bed and leaned his head against the wall. Almost immediately, he felt his muscles loosening up and his limbs become almost too heavy to lift. It was as though the entire day was catching up to him at once. If not for the alertness in his brain, he might have fallen asleep right then and there.

It was thanks to that alertness that he heard something rattling in the other room. Clint's heart forced a jolt of energy through his body and he leapt off the bed. By the time he heard the noise again, he was standing with his back pressed up against the wall next to the bedroom door.

The rattle was coming from the back door of the house. Clint recognized it because those hinges made a particular squeak that he'd noticed on his way inside. He picked up the sound of the door scraping against the frame moments later so he waited to hear incoming footsteps before making his own presence known.

Clint drew his Colt and held it at the ready. When he heard light footsteps creeping through the house, he pictured in his mind where the new arrival was headed. Once the steps were in the room outside his door, he stepped into the doorway and pointed his gun toward whoever was there.

The first thing he saw was a pair of wide eyes glimmering in the shadows. The pale moonlight caught in those eyes and made them appear to sparkle like gems. Those eyes were covered soon after by a pair of thin, trembling hands before the person crumpled down into a ball and huddled on the floor.

"Don't shoot me. Please don't shoot me," came an unsteady voice muffled by the hands that covered the woman's face. "I don't want to die. Please don't shoot me."

Clint holstered his gun, but kept his hand near the holster as he approached the woman on the floor. "It's all right," he said cautiously. "I don't want to kill you."

Thick waves of hair covered her face as she looked up at him. Her skin seemed especially smooth in the moonlight and Clint could see the tears running down her cheeks. She instinctively scooted back a little when Clint walked up to her and knelt down to her level.

"Who are you?" he asked.

It took a lot for her to look at him, but she finally managed the task. "I used to live here. In this house."

"I'm sorry about coming in, but I thought it was empty."

"It is . . . now. I came back with my brother a month ago and he was killed by the men who live here now. I just wanted to get somewhere that's safe. I'm so scared."

Clint sat down beside her and smoothed the hair away from her eyes. "Does anyone know you're here?"

"I don't think so. The rest of the ones who were captured are gone now. I thought I could catch up with them and get out but . . ."

"I can arrange for you to get out of here. For now, we both need some rest."

"My bed is still in the other room. We didn't take it with us when we cleared out the first time." Moving in closer to him, she leaned her head on Clint's shoulder "Will you hold me if I let you rest with me? I feel so safe next to you."

"Getting some rest does sound good. What's your name?"

She looked at him with wide, grateful eyes and said, "Paula."

THIRTY-EIGHT

Even though the bed was only one short step away from falling apart completely, it felt like a blessing against Clint's tired body. Paula laid down beside him, resting her arm over Clint's chest and her head on his shoulder. She'd undressed down to her slip and didn't seem at all uncomfortable laying with him there in the dark. In fact, she made contented little sounds as she worked her way in as close to him as she could get.

"This is the best I've felt since I can remember," she said.

"Me too." Surprisingly enough, Clint wasn't just talking when he said that. Even in the middle of the rat's nest, it felt damn good to get off his feet and close his eyes for a second. His brain was still pulling in all the sounds and sensations he could handle, but he'd gotten used to the constant alertness in a strange sort of way.

Paula's hand moved over his chest and slipped beneath the front of his shirt where the buttons had come unfastened during the day. She slipped her fingers beneath his clothing until even more of the buttons came loose. From there, she caressed his bare skin and started crawling on top of him.

"What are you doing?" Clint asked.

She smiled down at him and pulled his shirt open. "I don't know why, but I feel so close to you. After being afraid for so long and then finding you here I feel like I want to be close to you." Reaching down to take hold of Clint's hand, she guided him until he cupped one of her small, pert breasts. "I want you to be close to me. I want you to touch me and show me that I'm still alive."

Clint didn't resist her as she moved his hand over her body. When his fingertip grazed the top of her slip, he pulled the material down until it slid off her shoulder. Paula let out a satisfied moan and tilted her head back as Clint sat up and started moving his hands without her guidance.

The way she was sitting on top of him, Paula was straddling Clint's waist. She could feel him getting harder through his pants and began slowly rocking on top of him to spur him along. By this time, Clint was pulling the slip up over her head and tossing the garment to the floor. He couldn't get his hands off of her, even if he'd wanted to. Paula's skin was so soft and inviting that he wanted nothing more than to feel it pressed against every inch of himself.

It became obvious that she was thinking along those same lines as she tore Clint's shirt the rest of the way off and immediately went to work on his belt buckle so she could climb once again onto his naked body. Her skin was warm and wet against his and when she leaned down, she let her hair dangle forward and trace a soft pattern along his skin.

Clint could feel the urgent way she touched him and the insistence in her arms and legs. It almost seemed as though she was trying to grab hold of him tight enough to make sure he wouldn't get away. Watching her face and the way she moved, he began to feel the passion that flowed through her. It was a struggle, but he kept his senses attuned to what was going on within the rest of the house as he allowed himself to be swept away by Paula's infectious passion.

Her hands drifted between his legs while Clint nibbled on her neck and worked his mouth down to her breasts. Paula leaned back a little, making it easier for Clint to taste her little nipples while she began stroking his cock.

"Yes," she moaned. "God, you're so hard." With that, she lifted herself up and moved her wet pussy over the head of his penis. She spread her legs open to fit him in and lowered herself down, letting out a shuddering breath as she was filled up by his hard shaft.

Clint was taken a bit by surprise when he felt how insistently she rode on top of him. When Paula began riding the length of his cock, she did so with a desperate kind of strength while clamping her hands around his arms for support.

It was a surprise, but a very pleasant one.

Clint moved his hands down along her sides and rested them on her hips. When she moved on top of him, he felt the motion of her body and the way her muscles reacted as he drove deeper and deeper inside. When he began pumping into her even harder, she gripped him tighter and had to bite down on her lip to keep from making any noise.

She moved just the way she wanted, riding his shaft and grinding against it so that he rubbed against her most sensitive spots. Just as she got into a rhythm, Paula felt Clint moving beneath her and taking hold of her between his strong hands.

"What are you doing?" she asked breathlessly.

Clint didn't answer. Instead, he got out from beneath her and set her onto the bed. Still without saying a word, he moved around behind her and ran his hands over her sides. His chest pressed against her back and his cock slipped down over her buttocks and between her legs as he reached around to cup both of her breasts with his hands.

Paula tried to speak again. This time, however, her breathing was so intense that she had to struggle to get the words out. "What are you . . . oh . . . that . . . feels so . . ."

Rubbing her breasts so that her erect nipples brushed along his palms, Clint moved his hands to her shoulders and gently urged her to lean forward. She didn't resist in the slightest and grabbed hold of the edge of the mattress, moaning in anticipation as Clint moved his penis between her warm thighs.

Clint ran the tips of his fingers down over her shoulders and along the curve of her spine. He could feel her trembling as he worked his way down and she let out a soft groan when he eased his hands onto her hips. From there, he pushed forward and slid inside of her.

Paula arched her back and tossed her head back, causing her hair to land in a cascade over her shoulders. She breathed even heavier when Clint began pumping inside of her, clawing at the mattress as waves of pleasure began surging through her flesh.

The feel of Paula's body enclosing him made it hard for Clint to think about anything else but thrusting into her again and again. But when he considered that there might be danger lurking nearby or even closing in on him from outside, it made the moment seem even more enticing. The lurking threat added a spice to the already thrilling sensations he was feeling and made him want to savor those feelings even more.

Reaching out with one hand, Clint slipped his fingers through Paula's hair and made a fist. He could hear her gasp when he started pulling her head back gently while still pounding into her from behind. She reached out while turning to look back at him, her mouth open with a moan that she somehow kept from spilling out.

This time, Clint could see the surprise in her eyes. She was no longer in control of what was going on and although it had made her feel uncomfortable at first, she was only too happy to give in to him now. He locked eyes with her and pounded into her with an extra bit of strength, driving his cock in as deep as it could go.

Paula started to cry out, but managed to turn it into a kind of throaty growl that wouldn't be heard outside in the quiet remains of the town. Her body lost all of its tension as the first hints of an orgasm started tingling beneath her flesh.

Clint pulled her hair a little bit more, letting her know what he wanted her to do. Taking his lead without question, she straightened her back and placed her hands flat against the wall behind the bed. He had to lift her up a little, but still managed to keep inside of her as he pressed himself against her back.

From that angle, all Clint had to do was grind his hips against her and drive inside of her with quick, gentle thrusts. In a matter of seconds, Paula was gripped in the clutches of an orgasm that became even more powerful by the fact that she had to keep from making a noise as the pleasure tore through her system.

When she climaxed, Paula clenched around Clint's penis and held on tight, sending him over the edge himself. Clint wrapped his arms around her and thrust into her one last time before exploding powerfully inside of her.

They stayed in that position for a few moments, unable and unwilling to move. Finally, their bodies could no longer support them and they lowered themselves down onto the mattress. Although she was hesitant to let him slip out from between her legs, Paula held on tightly to him and pressed her breasts against his chest.

Clint laid there with her against him, sensing a definite change in the way she was then as opposed to the way she'd been when he'd found her. She seemed stronger somehow and completely at ease despite how afraid she'd been before.

Rather than let himself worry about it too much, Clint closed his eyes and let himself relax for the first time in what felt like days. His sleep was far from deep, but even though he could still hear what was going on around him as if from a distance, it was still restful.

He drifted off without really allowing himself to become unconscious. All the while, he made sure to pay close attention to the woman in his arms. He wasn't about to let anything happen to her without putting up a fight.

THIRTY-NINE

Even if Clint had wanted to stay awake, he wouldn't have been able to keep his body moving. He'd taxed himself too far and pushed himself too hard to keep himself going much longer without taking a break. He was able to force himself to wake up, but only after a few much-needed hours of sleep.

Clint sat straight up and quickly gathered up his clothes. Paula was still laying on the bed and he didn't let himself even think about her until he was fully dressed and had his gun belt buckled around his waist. By that time, she was beginning to stir.

"Here," Clint said while tossing her clothes onto the bed. "Put those on and get ready. We're leaving."

"But . . . it's not even daylight yet. Can't we—"

"No," Clint said sharply. "Whatever you were going to say, we can't do it. All we can do is get ready and leave. We're not safe here."

She looked like she wanted to say something, but kept it to herself. Instead, she pulled on her clothes and sat with her legs hanging off the side of the bed.

After checking out the house and surrounding area, Clint went back to her side. "I didn't mean for us to stay

159

put so long, that's all. We need to keep moving because it's only a matter of time before they find us."

"I know." Already, some of the hurt was draining from her eyes and she even managed to smile. "It's just that after last night, I wish the rest of the world would go away and just leave you and me."

"I know what you mean," Clint said. "But until that happens, there's something I want you to do for me."

"What's that?"

"Tell me where to find Alonzo Mason."

"I don't know. I never saw him, I was just—"

"A prisoner?" Clint's tone had shifted from calm and soothing to sharp and commanding. "Spare me that line, Paula. It wasn't too convincing when you first said it and it doesn't hold up much better now."

Her eyes narrowed slightly and she pulled her knees up close to her chest. "Clint, I don't know what you mean. Please, don't talk to me like that."

Clint's hand drifted down to rest upon the handle of his Colt. In one swift action, he drew the weapon and placed the muzzle against her hip. He kept his eyes locked onto hers as he slowly wrapped his finger around the trigger and started to squeeze.

"You're working for him," Clint whispered. "I may like to believe in coincidences sometimes, but you finding me here is too big a one for me to swallow. Besides, for someone so scared, you seemed awfully comfortable last night."

Her eyes darted between Clint's face and the gun in his hand.

"Besides," he continued, "why would some escaped prisoner bother coming back here? There's hardly anything left. And why aren't you squirming more . . ." The Colt's hammer dropped, making a metallic *click*. ". . . unless you knew this gun was empty?"

At that moment, a shadow seemed to lift from Paula's

face. All the fear was gone, but there was still a fair amount of tension left behind. "I didn't have a choice. And last night was . . ." She let the sentence trail off as she closed her eyes. A sly, naughty smile drifted across her lips and she pulled in a luxurious breath. "Last night was—"

"Save it," Clint said, already in the process of taking bullets from his gun belt and sliding them into the Colt's cylinder. "I want you to take me to Mr. Mason so I can get a look at the man responsible for a twisted place like this."

Nodding, Paula said, "Sure. I was supposed to bring you to him anyway. I just didn't think you'd want to go on your own."

Clint snapped the cylinder shut and waved the gun toward the door. "Just start walking."

She walked toward him with a catlike saunter. When she got almost close enough to touch him, Clint backed off a step and waved her through. Shrugging, Paula walked out of the bedroom and started walking through the front door.

Clint stayed behind her, ready for her to do or say anything that might be considered suspicious. Of course, everything she'd done from the moment he'd started having his doubts about her was considered suspicious.

"Can I ask you a question?" she asked while walking down the steps leading from the front porch to the street. Even though he didn't answer her, Paula kept on talking. "If you knew about me, then why did you take me to bed last night?"

"It's the best way I knew to keep you close, in my sight and out of trouble. Besides, there wasn't any place for you to hide a weapon where I couldn't see."

"Are those the only reasons?"

"You seemed anxious enough. Who was I to resist?"

Paula smiled and stepped down from the last step. From

there, she moved around to lean against the front of the
house as Clint walked down the steps. She still looked at
him with a certain kind of hunger and an attraction that
grew with every second. "When this is over should I come
find you again?"

"Sure," Clint said. "You do that."

He stepped down onto the ground and turned to keep
Paula in his sight. As soon as she winked at him, Clint
knew there was going to be trouble. Paula's hand was
placed flat against the wall and she leaned on it just
slightly.

There was a muted thump that Clint could feel through
the bottom of his boots more than he could hear it. His
hand went reflexively for the Colt, but it was already too
late. The ground he'd been standing on gave way as a
pair of swinging trapdoors were unlocked beneath his feet.

Even as he started to fall, Clint managed to draw the
Colt and bring it up. His lower body had already gone
down into the hole that had suddenly appeared. His lower
back scraped along the edge of the hole as he kept falling
and he reached out reflexively to try and stop himself with
his hands.

By that time, he was almost inside. Clint's brain raced
frantically for what he should do next. He felt as though
time had slowed around him and he could feel his descent
as though he was being lowered at the end of a rope rather
than in free fall. No matter how many things he thought
of doing, it was too late to finish any of them.

His feet scraped along the back of the hole and then
his entire world became flooded with pain, the sound of
blood rushing through his head and encroaching darkness.
The base of Clint's skull clipped the edge of the hole,
which was lined with wood to keep the edges nice and
crisp.

With his own falling weight behind the impact, it felt

as though Clint had been hit with a sledgehammer.

Blinding, fiery pain coursed through his head and surged all the way down his spine. He was blacking out by the time it would have reached his legs.

When his body landed in a pile at the bottom of the hole, he was completely unconscious.

Paula took her hand away from the panel she'd activated in the wall. Apart from the tunnels and doors Mason had installed, he'd also littered the town with traps like the one Clint had just found. That was how he'd managed to win out over so many other intruders in the past.

She stepped over to the side of the hole and looked in. When she looked up again, Luke was already on his way.

FORTY

The next time Clint's eyes opened, he was hanging from the underside of a cellar door. There were vague recollections of how he'd gotten there drifting through his head, but it took him a while to focus enough for him to know those weren't just dreams.

He could recall floating from one place to another with what felt like a stone pressing against the soft part of his gut. He could remember light turning into dark and the smell of fresh air becoming dirtier and filled with the musty odor of dust.

After he'd had some time to think about it, Clint realized that those sensations had been his memory of being pulled out of the hole, slung over someone's shoulder and carried to wherever he was now. He'd been locked away out of the light and tossed someplace underground.

There was the *clank* of iron rings being fitted into place around his wrists and the metallic *click* of a lock being snapped shut to hold the rope around his neck at just the right tension. As far as where he was, what type of contraption he was in and what was going to happen to him, Clint had figured all of that out on his own. After all, he'd had plenty of time to think for the first day, since his captors seemed to have forgotten he was even there.

With no way to move and no strength to break free, Clint had diverted all his energy to keeping his eyes open and soaking up every last detail he could find. In that respect, all the practice he'd given himself before in using all his senses at once came in extra handy. There were times when the light shining from behind him was just enough to reflect against the dust particles that constantly swirled in the stagnant air. And there were other times when he was forced to give himself a rest and let his head sag forward, causing the rope to tighten and the blood to pound through his ears.

He kept track of time by watching the shadows on the floor. Actually, it was more helpful to watch the intensity of the light that managed to filter in between the boards of the door above him. Never before had time seemed to drag so slowly. Every second was a fight to survive as well as a fight to figure a way out of that damn cellar.

Toward the middle of the second day, Clint noticed that the contraption holding him to the door, although very well constructed, wasn't entirely without its weaknesses. It was made of wood, and wood could be splintered, warped or snapped. The rings were made of metal, which just might be able to help that snapping process along.

For the rest of that day and the better part of the next, Clint had begun the process of doing what little he could to wear away at the structure that held him back. At first, all he could really do was twist his hands within the iron rings. That alone was enough to peel away several layers of his skin without making much of a dent in the shackles themselves.

Just as he'd been about to give up, he heard that subtle squeaking sound, followed by the distinctive noise of wood giving way. It wasn't the victorious crack that he'd been hoping for, but it was enough to let him know that he was indeed on the right track.

If he'd believed in higher powers watching over him,
he would have easily taken the sound as a sign to keep
up what he was doing. And in much the same way that
every man with his head in a noose suddenly learned to
pray, Clint started believing that there might just be something or someone looking over him. At least thinking that
made it easier for him to keep working through the pain
and keep straining his muscles time and again even
though his strength was all but gone.

As if it wasn't bad enough that he was strung up to die
and abandoned in a dark, forgotten cellar, the third day
was when he truly started to feel his body yearning for
food and water. Any man who traveled on his own had
to tough it out through a lean patch if he ran into trouble
on the trail or was forced to find shelter in a cruel climate.
Any man in those situations knew what it was like to feel
his gut twisting around on itself and his throat begin to
crack from dryness. It was a necessary thing sometimes
and one of the best ways to get through it was to not
dwell on what you were missing.

But Clint wasn't just in a cruel environment. He was
in a dungeon where he couldn't let his head droop forward
or even take the weight off his feet. He'd been standing
up for three days and the back of his head still felt as
though it was cracked open. Hell . . . for all he knew, it
was cracked open after taking that fall.

All of that would have been hard enough to take, but
things only got worse when that bastard with the shovel
decided to poke his head into Clint's dungeon and stir up
the pot a bit. That skinny rat of a man sat on his rickety
stool and chewed on his nails as though it was a hobby.

And all the while, Rat-man didn't take his eyes off of
Clint. He stared at him, waiting, while gnawing on the
ends of his fingers and spitting the slivers out onto the
floor. He stared and waited as though he didn't want to
take the chance of witnessing the exact moment when

Clint's life was snuffed out after fighting to hold on for so long.

As if reading Clint's thoughts, Rat-man took his index finger out of his mouth, spat out a piece of nail and said, "Ain't nobody held out this long. What you waitin' for, anyway? You think someone's coming for ya?"

Clint tensed his muscles and relaxed, tensed and relaxed, while breathing in his slow, haggard rhythm.

"Nobody even knows you're here," Rat-man continued. "Well, let's just say the ones who do know ain't about to do nothin' about it." That seemed to amuse him a little and a wiry grin slithered onto his face.

"Where's Paula?" Clint asked. That question was the only thing that he ever said to Rat-man apart from the occasional colorful request that came out automatically every once in a while.

The other man's beady eyes narrowed and he bared a set of crooked teeth. "I told you before not to worry about her. I don't even want to hear you mention her name once more or—"

"Or what?"

Even locked to the underside of a cellar door, Clint could back the smaller man off with just a certain look. Shuffling back to his stool, Rat-man stuck his fingers back in his mouth and Clint got back to work on his own task.

FORTY-ONE

The sun had stopped beating down on Clint's back through the gaps in the door long enough for him to know that it was getting to be the end of the fourth day. He couldn't feel his legs anymore, but somehow managed to keep them from buckling. Looking down, he saw that his feet were cocked at odd angles, propping him up more on their sides rather than flat against the ground.

Rat-man had left him alone for a while, probably to get some food and sleep before taking up his vigil again. The only parts of Clint's body that still had definite feeling were his hands and neck, and that was only because of the constant pain that flowed through them.

He didn't have to consciously think about flexing the muscles in his arms anymore. They just went through the repeated motions as if that's all they'd ever done. As much as he'd hated to admit it, however, the rope around his neck was simply not going to break before he was strangled to death.

It was all he could do to keep his head up, which meant that straining against the rope was pretty much out of the realm of possibility. If the loop had given way a little sooner, he might have had a chance against it, but so much of the skin beneath his chin had been sheared away that even touching the rope sent spikes of agony up and down his body. That rope was slick with his own blood and reeked of the gore's coppery scent.

In his mind, Clint could hear that metallic *click* of a lock fitting into place. He knew now that the rope must somehow have been pulled through the mechanism and then locked into place. Without the key, Clint wasn't about to get free of that noose. In fact, he was lucky that he'd loosened it enough to give himself some slack.

He wasn't sure what else he could do at that point. If there was someone in charge to talk to, he might have been able to bargain his way out. Rat-man obviously wasn't calling the shots and wasn't even smart enough to engage in real conversation anyway. That was probably why he'd been chosen for the duty of guarding Clint; all the scrawny weasel knew how to do was chew his nails and use a shovel.

If he could get even a part of his body free, he might be able to fight his way out. But the way he was feeling, Clint wondered if he would even be able to stand on his own if the restraints were somehow taken away.

Hunger and thirst was ravaging him on the inside, and in a matter of time, those factors alone would cause him a slow, horrible death.

Plenty of times Clint Adams had been in scrapes where any other man might not have come out alive. Although all those times had been close, some closer than others, he'd always found a way out. Either his brain could figure some way to cheat the Reaper or his reflexes were quick enough to buy him some time.

This time, however, Clint was starting to wonder if he was too late to do much of anything except let himself relax and give in. He'd had a good, long run and had even made a name for himself. He'd done good by a lot of people and there were plenty of folks out there who were still alive thanks to him.

Hanging there in the dark, stinking cellar, which only stank more with every passing day, Clint couldn't help but wonder what it would be like to die. The thought wasn't a pleasant one and he certainly didn't welcome its presence within his consciousness, but it was there all the same.

He looked down and saw his feet, propping him up at their odd angles and couldn't help but smile. At least he still had his boots on. There was some comfort to be taken from that.

A part of him told him to close his eyes and let himself rest. Not for long. Just for a second or two, maybe a minute. After going for so long without any sleep or comfort of any kind, the notion of letting his body go slack for just a little bit was starting to make more and more sense.

Clint's head began to slump forward, but he was woken up by a jolt of pain shooting through his neck. Reflexively, his whole body tensed as though he was going to catch himself while falling. His arms jerked forward and his back twisted against the mechanism that held him in place.

At that moment, he heard something that not only woke him up all the way, but showed him a light at the end of his tunnel.

When his arms had tensed that last time, Clint pulled against the iron rings with more force than he'd been able to manage in some time. With that, the rings creaked in their settings until there was a distinctive snap.

Clint remained perfectly still, like a man who wasn't sure if he was dreaming or not but didn't want the feeling to end. He moved his left arm and found that it couldn't go any farther than before. The right arm was next and

when he moved that one, he felt the iron ring bend outward.

It took some effort, but he was able to move the ring
even farther. The pain shooting through him was enough
to blur his vision with dark spots, but he kept on twisting
until there was another snap of splintering wood.

The blood in Clint's veins began to pump and some
feeling started to return to his legs. Even his feet scraped
against the floor, righting themselves until he was no
longer pressing down on the sides of his ankles like some
kind of cripple.

Every time he moved his right arm now, he could hear
the rings working their way through their wooden settings.
Each creak was music to his ears and although the blood
was once again trickling down his arm, the warmth made
him feel more alive than he had in days.

He wanted to keep working his way through the restraints while he still had the strength, but when Clint took
a break to catch his breath he heard another sound that
made him stop what he was doing. This sound was much
more familiar than the first, although he'd only heard it
once or twice before.

It was the sound of someone coming down to the cellar.
There was the thump of footsteps against the dirt floor as
well as the clatter of doors being opened and closed.
Those footsteps were different than what he'd heard when
Rat-man came and went; they were different because there
was more than one person making them. By the sound of
it, there were at least three.

Clint stopped straining against the iron ring right when
he thought he might break through. He wanted to see who
was coming.

FORTY-TWO

Clint focused his eyes on the entrance to the cellar with such intensity that he could almost feel heat radiating from his eyes. He'd seen Rat-man come and go enough times that he knew which direction the door was although he couldn't see it from where he was hanging.

The first person to step into view was the rodentlike figure that Clint had become so familiar with over the last couple of days. The skinny guard still held his shovel over his shoulder. This time, however, the smile on his face was at least twice as wide as it had ever been.

When Rat-man stepped into the cellar and walked over to his usual spot in the corner, he looked at Clint as though he was taking in the colors of the sunset. The morbid little bastard damn near licked his lips as he stuck the shovel's blade into the dirt and leaned against its splintered wooden shaft.

Next through the door was a lean, muscular figure with short-cropped black hair and a gun strapped around his waist. His were the weary eyes of a killer, which Clint could recognize even after all he'd been through. The dark-haired man walked inside and made his way to the opposite corner of where Rat-man was standing. Apparently, he liked the skinny man with the shovel just as much as Clint did.

Unable to keep his silence another moment, Rat-man looked over to the other gunman and started to laugh. "Which one of us gets to kill him, Luke? I'll let you if you really wa—"

"Ellis," the other man said. "Shut up."

Even though he now knew the man with the shovel had a real name, Clint couldn't put the word *Ellis* to that face. Rat-man was so much more fitting and that was how he would still think of him.

Luke kept his eyes on Ellis for another second before turning to look at Clint. There was no anger or hatred in his gaze, just the cold, calculating stare of a hunter. The only thing that was probably going through Luke's mind was how many shots it would take to put Clint down.

The footsteps from outside were still coming. Stepping through the door and moving through the cellar holding a lantern in one hand, Paula walked between the other two men and hung her lantern from a hook in the ceiling. She took a moment to adjust the knob until the flame was bright enough to illuminate the musty room without giving off too much of a glare.

Once that was done, she walked straight across the room until she was standing directly in front of Clint. Paula kept silent, looking at him as though she expected him to have something to say. When Clint didn't do anything besides look back at her, she stepped up a little closer until he was able to smell the familiar scent of her skin.

"Ellis told me you were asking to see me," she said in a smooth, controlled voice. Even though she spoke in an even tone, there was something about the way she held her jaw that seemed odd. It seemed as though she might have been hurt recently and didn't want to aggravate anything by moving too much.

When Clint tried to speak, his words became snagged on a dry crack in the middle of his throat. He coughed up just enough to enable his voice to be heard and said, "I was asking where you were."

"And why is that?"

"Because I figured you'd be right next to this Mr. Mason I've heard about. Also I wanted to congratulate you."

Paula smiled. "Really?"

This time, Clint saw for sure that she was speaking through clenched teeth. "Yeah. That was one hell of a setup job you pulled. I was even watching for you to do something."

"I know. And that's the most satisfying time to pull something over on someone."

Despite the pain in his neck, Clint shook his head. "You're a real bitch, you know that?"

"I didn't figure you for the crude type, Clint."

"I must be overly tired."

"Well, let's see if this helps you liven up a bit."

After saying that, Paula leaned forward and reached out to place her hands on either side of Clint's face. From there, she kissed Clint on the lips with almost as much passion as she'd had when they were in the same bed.

Not one part of Clint responded to the kiss. Instead, all he did was glare into her closed eyes and keep his face as rigid as stone.

But that didn't stop Paula. Her lips moved over his, ignoring the fact that she was the only one doing any work. Suddenly, her eyes opened and she returned Clint's stare. Her tongue slipped from between her lips and pressed against Clint's.

Clint responded out of sheer surprise when he felt the cool touch of metal against his lower lip. He opened his mouth as if to speak and Paula slid her tongue all the way inside. After a tense couple of seconds, she moved her lips until they grazed against Clint's ear.

"He's coming to see you die," she whispered quickly. "No matter what he says or tells you, these are the only men he's got."

"That's enough, Paula," came Luke's voice from the other side of the room. "What are you saying to him?"

She stepped back and flashed a serpentine smile while opening her mouth and licking her lips. "I told him that nobody calls me a bitch and lives to see the next day."

"That's true enough," came a voice that sounded vaguely familiar, but only in a distorted kind of way. The man who'd just spoken entered the cellar and took his time getting close enough for Clint to get a look at him. When he stepped into the room itself, he stopped and locked eyes with the man who hung from the underside of the cellar door.

"Morgan?" Clint asked in a voice that sounded as though his tongue had started to swell. "Is that you?"

The man standing in front of him looked exactly the same as the man Clint had met in the saloon when he'd first arrived, although he carried himself completely differently. Rather than look afraid or meek, this man stood up tall, threw back his broad shoulders and carried himself like royalty.

"Morgan's a man I keep in the back of my head when I can't be Alonzo Mason. But yes, I played that part when you first arrived. But it's Mason who's going to watch you die."

FORTY-THREE

"Actually," Mason said as he strutted close enough to get a better look at Clint's face in the flickering light of the hanging lantern, "I'm glad you've held out this long. I thought I might not get the chance to see you again."

"We're headed out tomorrow," Ellis said. "Ain't that right, Mr. Mason?"

"That's right. This town holds a special place in my heart, but it's time for me to move to another, bigger town so I can expand my sphere of influence. I was thinking somewhere in Wyoming or Colorado. Of course, this town will still be mine. After all, I rebuilt it into an image entirely my own."

"Yeah," Clint said through clenched teeth. "Real nice rat's nest you've got here."

Suddenly, Mason's eyes flared and his face became a mask of pure hatred. "I built this town. How dare you call it that!"

"You didn't build a damn thing. You waited until it was empty and you burrowed around inside of it just like a rat."

"You see why I wanted to put you here? Luke over there said we should just shoot you while you were

176

knocked out, but I would have none of that. After you killed so many of my men, I wanted you to suffer before you died." When he said those words, a grim smile replaced the seething anger on Mason's face. "And I can see you've suffered plenty.

"When we move out of this state, me and all my men will find us another place to call home and those who follow after me can use this as a place of refuge for a price of course. The Underground Railroad was such a nice idea I don't see any reason to abandon it. Especially since there are so many out there willing to pay for such a service."

Clint let out a pained breath. "You're insane."

"Really? How do you figure?"

"I see it in your eyes."

"Well, this crazy man is going to be rich before too long. And this crazy man is also the same man who managed to do what so many others could not. I've taken the life of Clint Adams. The Gunsmith himself will perish beneath my own streets where he will be forgotten and," he added, looking over to Ellis, "buried."

Clint looked over the other man from head to toe. His eyes moved in his skull, soaking up the details in less than a second. It was amazing how fast he could work when his life depended on it.

Mason was dressed as though he was on his way to a ball. His pearl-gray pants matched his vest, and were only a shade lighter than the coat he wore, which came down past his knees. There was a watch chain hanging over his stomach and his hair was perfectly plastered down into place by some kind of sweet-smelling oil.

What interested Clint the most was the leather gun belt strapped around his waist. By the looks of it, that holster hadn't seen more than the occasional use and was probably only for show. It held a .44 revolver, which was polished well enough to fit in with the rest of Mason's outfit.

"So that's it?" Clint asked. "You want to move on, clean out another town and hollow that one out as well?"

"Not clean it out. Merely modify it so it can become the next stop in my own Underground Railroad."

"Oh. My mistake," Clint said. "I still think you're insane, though."

Mason shook his head. "Whatever you think, it doesn't matter. You're a dead man, Adams. You have no voice."

Clint's eyes narrowed and he spoke in a tense hiss. "Say that to my face, you crazy son of a bitch."

Only too happy to oblige, Mason sauntered forward until he was standing less than a foot or two away from Clint. Once there, he lowered his head as though he was talking to a child and kept his eyes fixed squarely on Clint's. "I said, you are a—"

Clint pulled up all of his strength, adding to it every ounce of frustration, pain and anger that had been building up over the last four days. He channeled all of that power into his right arm, which he snapped forward hard enough to tear the iron ring out of its wooden anchor and toss it to the floor in a noisy clatter.

His hand kept right on moving, dropping down to snatch the fancy-looking .44 from Mason's holster and bring it up while snapping back the trigger.

"Dead man," Clint said, finishing the taunt that Mason himself had started.

FORTY-FOUR

Luke was already starting to draw his weapon, but Clint took aim and fired once before the other man could clear leather. Clint's shot blasted Luke through the chest. Just to make sure, Clint aimed and fired again, drilling a second hole through the gunman's heart.

Still holding his gun in hand, Luke straightened up and fell over, his gun spitting a wild shot into the wall.

Mason was already reeling back, trying to put as much distance as possible between himself and the newly armed prisoner. "Kill him! Kill him," he shouted toward Ellis.

The skinny man tightened his grip around the handle of his shovel and shook himself out of the shock that had caused him to freeze when Clint had made his lethal move. Now, Rat-man lifted the shovel, cocked it back over his shoulder and began to charge toward Clint with a shrill scream building in the back of his throat.

Clint opened his right hand and dropped the gun to the floor. He then reached into his mouth and pulled out the small key that had been slipped to him through Paula's kiss. Until that moment, he'd stuffed the key beneath his tongue. The moment he took it out, he reached up for the spot where he'd seen someone reach in one of his vague

179

dreams of being locked up in the first place.

Using his instinct and trusting his hazy memory, Clint found the keyhole after missing only once. With one twist of his wrist, the mechanism opened and the whole thing swung open like a gallows. The iron ring on his left hand moved away and the rope around his neck loosened and fell to the floor.

Clint dropped straight down just in time to avoid getting his face smashed in by the blade of the shovel in Ratman's hands. While squatting down, he swept up the gun and jabbed it up into Ellis's stomach.

Ellis looked down with a dumb, questioning look on his face that turned to surprised horror when Clint pulled the trigger. One muffled *thump* was followed by another, and the two bullets threw the skinny man back as though he was being dragged behind a cart.

He didn't know quite how he found the strength, but Clint managed to stand up and walk slowly toward Mason.

"Kill me and you'll die next," Mason said. "The rest of my men are out there and they'll gun you down. Hand over my gun and I'll tell them to let you go."

Clint kept walking forward, savoring every moment that Mason used to bargain and back away.

"You don't have the strength to fight them all, Adams. You do have my word, though. I'll let you leave this town if you hand me my gun." Mason actually sounded as though he was regaining his confidence. The more words he got out of his mouth, the more of his royal demeanor came back to him.

"Be reasonable," Mason said in a tone that dripped with honey. He held out his hand and said, "I admire you as a fighter. You're a true warrior. That's the only reason you can rely on my word as a gentleman. I'll give the order for my men to let you go. Kill me, and they'll shoot you on sight."

"Fine," Clint said as he spun the pistol around so that he could place its handle in Mason's outstretched hand. "Give your order."

Mason smiled widely and looked over his shoulder. "Men," he shouted. "Let Mister Adams leave unmolested."

Clint nodded and started to walk toward the door. Before his back was fully to the other man, Clint heard Mason shift on his feet and snap back the hammer of the .44. Clint spun as well, catching Mason's wrist before he could take aim and twisting the finely dressed man's hand around until the .44 was pointed up at Mason's own chin.

The .44 went off before Mason had a chance to say another word in his own defense. The bullet that had been meant for Clint's back cleared a path through Mason's skull instead, wiping the smirk completely off his face.

Clint stuck the pistol beneath his belt and looked around for Paula. He found her huddled in a corner, far away from where all the bullets had been flying.

"Why did you do that?" Clint asked.

She stepped out of the shadows and walked up to him with her hands crossed over her chest. "Do what?"

"Give me the key? Why did you do that?"

"If you would have let me finish talking back at my old house, you might already know the answer."

Clint had to think for a moment, but then remembered that she'd started to say something that he hadn't let her finish. God, that seemed like another lifetime ago. "What did you want to tell me?"

"I wanted to tell you that the night we spent together was . . . the first time anyone's made me feel like a woman and not an object. It was like you lit a fire inside me, Clint Adams."

"Is that why you tossed me down that hole?"

"No. Mason would have killed me if I didn't do my part. But that was why I decided to help you afterward. I couldn't have lived with myself if I let a man like you die in a place like this."

She reached out to place her hand on his face. Slowly, she moved in front of him and kissed him on the cheek. It was a gentle kiss and when she moved to his mouth, she merely caressed his lips with her own, keeping herself mindful of the cuts and bruises on his face.

"I'm telling the first lawman I find about this place," Clint told her. "Do yourself a favor and leave here before that happens. In return, I need a horse as well as my gun."

"No problem. But before you go, I want you to kiss me like you did that night. Even if you don't mean it."

Clint wrapped his arms around her and kissed her passionately on the mouth. He wasn't about to tell her but he most definitely meant it.

Clint felt every bump in the road during his ride to the cabin where he was to meet the people he'd helped get out from under Mason's thumb. When he finally found the place, Clint thought everyone had already gone their separate ways. There was no sign of life until the front door opened and a familiar shape filled up the entire opening.

"It's about time you showed," Bo said as he waved a massive hand toward Clint. "Your horse has been getting awful restless."

"Thanks for keeping an eye on him."

"The others have moved on, but I figured I owed it to you to wait a bit longer. What went on in that place?" Once Clint got a little closer, Bo's face twisted and he said, "You look like hell. How do you feel?"

Clint looked up at the open sky and pulled in a deep breath of fresh air. "I feel good," he said as Eclipse came trotting around from where he'd been grazing behind the cabin. "I feel damn good."

Watch for

A KILLER'S HANDS

259th novel in the exciting GUNSMITH series
from Jove

Coming in July!

J. R. ROBERTS

THE GUNSMITH

LONGARM

**Explore the exciting Old West with one
of the men who made it wild!**